PROTECTED BY THE COMPANION: A REGENCY ROMANCE

LADIES ON THEIR OWN: GOVERNESSES AND COMPANIONS (BOOK 5)

ROSE PEARSON

PROTECTED BY THE COMPANION

Ladies on their Own: Governesses and Companions

(Book 5

By

Rose Pearson

© Copyright 2022 by Rose Pearson - All rights reserved.

In no way is it legal to reproduce, duplicate, or transmit any part of this document by either electronic means or in printed format. Recording of this publication is strictly prohibited and any storage of this document is not allowed unless with written permission from the publisher. All rights reserved.

Respective author owns all copyrights not held by the publisher.

PROTECTED BY THE COMPANION

PROLOGUE

"My Lord, you have an urgent letter."
Grimacing, Giles, Earl of Bargrave, rubbed at his eyes with the back of his hand. "It is far too early to be interrupted with such things."

His valet opened his mouth, began to stammer, and then closed it again. "My Lord... I...

"What time is it anyway?" As the drapes to his bedchamber were thrown back, Giles suddenly realized that it was not as early as he had first believed. The sun, it seemed, was very high in the sky, for it shone brightly through the window and made him wince. Little wonder the valet was stammering, given that he did not wish to disagree with Giles, whilst at the same time being fully aware that it was not as early as Giles had stated. Clearing his throat, Giles reluctantly pushed himself up into a sitting position. Holding one hand out to the valet, he snapped his fingers impatiently. "An urgent letter, you say?"

Scurrying over towards him at once, the valet held out a small piece of paper sealed with red wax.

"Yes, my Lord. The messenger arrived only fifteen

minutes ago and is insisting that he must return to his mistress at once, with your reply. The butler asked that I bring this to you immediately."

Giles arched an eyebrow as he turned his attention to the letter. *A lady? Why has a lady written to me so urgently?*

It was soon to be the Season and Giles had every intention of making his way to London. Whilst he had enjoyed a few dalliances the previous year, he was not a gentleman inclined to breaking the heart of any society lady. Neither would he ever touch a newly out young woman, or in any way risk the reputation of an unmarried young lady. The ladies he considered to be fine company were those widowed or those who sought company in the place of their philandering husbands. In such cases, Giles was only too happy to provide the comfort and security they needed. However, that would only ever be for a short time, and certainly would not continue beyond the Season. Was a particular lady eager to know if he would be returning to London soon, he wondered? So eager that she would write to him in advance of the Season even beginning?

"Have someone bring me coffee. Once I have dealt with this, I will call for you to assist me with my attire." Waving one hand at the valet, he dismissed him quickly. "And whatever the messenger may consider urgent, inform him that he is to have something to eat and a short respite before he will be permitted to return. I shall answer the letter, of course, but it will take a little time and I shall not act with any overwhelming urgency, unless it is completely merited."

Which I am not convinced it will be.

Being entirely disinclined to read such a letter in the company of his valet, Giles waited until the door to his bedchamber was closed before he permitted himself to even unfold it. If it was what he expected it to be, then the only urgency would be for him to have his response sent to the lady before the return of her husband, wherever he may be – and that would not take him long.

"Mayhap it is from Lady Brownlee."

Smiling to himself, he recalled the lady he had been particularly delighted with. *I should be glad indeed to have a letter from her.*

The moment his eyes fell upon the letter however, Giles found himself deeply frustrated. It was not from a particular lady as he had hoped. Instead, it was from none other than his sister. A sister whom he had not heard from in some time. A sister who had married a most distinguished gentleman, but who now lived very far away indeed on the west coast of Scotland. Giles did not begrudge her that choice, for the gentleman was to be admired amongst society. He was only disappointed that he had seen so very little of his only sibling, over the many years since her marriage, and during these last five years they had only ever spoken through letters.

'MY DEAR BROTHER,' the letter began, '*It is with great distress that I write to you. My dear husband has become unwell. The physician has been many times and whilst we are now convinced that he is over the worst, it will be many months before he can recover enough to make the journey from Scotland. As you are aware from my previous letter, our one and only daughter was to come to London this summer. She is greatly distressed at the thought of being unable to be there for the London Season, given that she has had new gowns purchased and the usual preparations made. She is, of course, greatly distressed over her father's illness, but now that he is recovering, there is a hope that she may still be able to attend.'*

Giles let out a huff of breath. Somehow, he seemed to sense what was coming... and already he knew his answer.

'You are our only hope, brother. I assume that you are to make your way to London for the Season as you do every year. Might you be willing to have your niece reside with you? Might you be willing to sponsor her into society? She will, of course, have a companion to chaperone her, so that you are not entirely pulled away from your own invitations and the like. You have no requirement to consent, but I beg of you – as her uncle and as my brother – to, at the very least, consider it. At least write to me that you are thinking of what you will do, rather than immediately refusing. I am all too aware of how much the London Season means to you but pray, consider putting yourself into a little more difficulty for your niece's sake.'

"And now I am to be made to feel guilty!"

After setting down the letter, Giles ran one hand through his fair hair, sending it in all directions. Guilt began to nudge at his soul but with an effort, Giles ignored it. He had a great deal to look forward to in the upcoming London Season! If he were to take on his niece, then such pleasures would be diminished.

"It is as my sister says - I have no requirement to agree." Taking a deep breath, he set his shoulders and gazed out across the room towards the window. "No. I need not agree. I will not take on my niece, companion or otherwise."

Setting back the covers, Giles threw out his legs and rose from his bed, ringing for the valet. Once the man arrived, Giles was dressed quickly and then settled at the small escritoire near the window to write to his sister. The note would be short and to the point, making it clear that he could not take his niece on.

Although I must make certain to include words of concern for my dear sister's husband. A slight frown pulled at Giles' brow. *I am a little anxious to hear that he has been so unwell. I should not want my sister to become a widow, nor my niece and nephew to become fatherless.*

He scowled to himself as he drew out a sheet of paper. All he wished for at present was to write his letter and then send the messenger back to his sister. Any delay might mean a change of mind, and Giles was determined not to give in. And yet, with every moment that passed, he found himself struggling to stand boldly behind his decision.

Thoughts of his broken-hearted niece entered his mind. A vision of his sister – upset and crying when she had already endured so much - soon followed. Rubbing one hand down his face, Giles shook his head to himself.

"It would mean the most dull Season for me." A slight shudder shook his frame. "I should have to give up so much – much of which I have been waiting for some time."

He would not be able to *entertain* as much as he might have liked. There would be responsibilities set upon his shoulders. Responsibilities which he did not want, for the London Season was an opportunity to forget all such obligations.

And yet, by the time Giles lifted the pen to write, his heart was so burdened with guilt that he could not stand by his original decision. His sister's plea had done as it intended.

Giles would be his niece's sponsor into society.

CHAPTER ONE

"And what is your uncle like?"

Miss Emma Lawder watched her charge carefully, seeing the way that Lady Juliet clutched both her hands together and looked out of the window.

"In truth, I do not know. I am not well acquainted with him."

"That is because you live in Scotland and he lives in England, I assume?"

"Yes, that is so. He has not often come to Scotland, and mother and father are less than inclined to travel such a long distance. We live so very far away and are very contented with the company that we *do* have."

Emma smiled softly, reached across, and pressed her hand to Lady Juliet's.

"My dear girl, you need not worry about London. I am aware that you are very happy with the circumstances at home, but you must find a situation of your own. How can you do so if you remain so far from society?" Lady Juliet shrugged one delicate shoulder and turned her head away. Sighing inwardly, Emma sat back, resting her head against the squabs. It did not seem to matter what she did or said, Lady Juliet remained upset at being forced to come from Scotland to London. "You have not made a promise to anyone at home, I hope?"

One lifted eyebrow was sent in Lady Juliet's direction, but the girl quickly shook her head, although a rosy glow came into her cheeks almost at once. Closing her eyes, Emma bit back a sharp response. It would do no good to berate her charge. She had not known the girl long, and such things were secret unless Lady Juliet wished to divulge them. No doubt an affectionate farmer's son or stable hand had made his attentions known and the girl had simply lapped them up.

"You must be careful in London. We cannot have every gentleman falling in love with you and you declaring yourself to them also. That would cause a great scandal."

"I have no intention of making every gentleman in London fall in love with me. In fact, I will remain quite silent, very dull, and so staid that they will stay far from me."

Lady Juliet kept her head turned towards the window, but Emma did not miss the slight lift of her chin as she spoke. Clearly the girl was rebelling against her forced departure to London, but Emma was quite certain that, within a sennight, Lady Juliet would be desperate to remain. All thought of home would be forgotten, and she would lose herself in the delights of London society.

Life as a chaperone was very different from life as Emma had experienced it thus far. Even now, she could still feel a lingering sense of shock over her father's sudden determination that she ought to leave his house to take up employment. At the very least, she had been able to choose her situation and had chosen Lady Juliet's house in Scotland, simply so that she might put as much distance between herself and her father as possible. Baron Wakefield had always been a disinterested father. Once her elder brother was wed and settled, her father had set his mind to finding a way to remove her from his house, seeing her as nothing more than a burden which must be removed from his shoulders as soon as possible.

Emma, who had never felt any sort of love or affection from her father, had not been surprised at such eagerness, although she had been deeply dismayed to learn that he wished her to become nothing more than a paid chaperone. She had believed that there might be an arrangement in her future; that her husband might be chosen for her, but never once had she thought that her father would push her into such a low situation. The last two months of residing at Lord and Lady Hyndford's estate had given her the opportunity to become used to such a position, although the strains of doing so still lingered over her heart. At times it was difficult to conceal her pain, knowing that she would never have a husband or a family to call her own; that she would never have the opportunity to be mistress of her own house - but concentrating all her efforts on Lady Juliet had helped that somewhat – and Emma was determined to continue to be devoted to the lady, as they entered the London Season.

"We must make sure that you behave well for your uncle. It is as your mother has said: he has given up a great deal to be your sponsor into society. I am not sure whether he even wished to come to London this Season!" Having never met the Earl of Bargrave, Emma had very little idea as to the sort of gentleman he might be. Lady Hyndford had spoken very highly of her brother, but Emma was always inclined to make her own judgments on a person's character. *However, I must think well of him for taking on his niece, at the very least!* A flutter of butterflies began to wave their wings in the pit of her stomach. As the carriage finally pulled to a stop. "I assume that we have arrived." Leaning forward to look out of the carriage window, Emma cleared her throat, put on the best smile that she could, and looked toward her charge. "You recall what your mother said to you, my dear?" Lady Juliet nodded, and Emma noticed how the rosy flush had begun to fade from her charge's cheeks. "You will greet your uncle properly," she reminded her, gently. "You will give him greetings from your mother and your father, and inform him of the letter that you have with you, from your mother. Make sure that we are nothing but thankfulness. Lord Bargrave deserves nothing less."

Her charge licked her lips, nodded, and then turned to face the carriage door. It had been a long drive and Emma herself was a little stiff, although she would not be able to truly stretch her limbs until she was in the comfort of her room. As Lady Juliet's companion, she could not expect the very best of rooms, but she was hopeful that it would be a lovely and restful place for her to reside. Lady Hyndford had been more than kind in that regard and, silently, Emma prayed that Lord Bargrave was of a similar ilk.

"I confess myself a little anxious." Whispering still, Lady Juliet turned a pale face towards Emma as, immediately, Emma put a comforting hand on her charge's shoulder. "I hope he will not be a hard-hearted sort."

"I am sure you need not worry."

Emma went to say more, but drew back her hand when the carriage door opened. She heard, rather than saw, Lady Juliet take a deep breath before she accepted the hand of the waiting footman and climbed down from the carriage. There came no exclamation of excitement nor delight, however, nor were there words of greeting from either Lady Juliet or her uncle. As Emma climbed down from the carriage, her hand grasping the footman's tightly, her eyes widened in astonishment.

The street was quite empty. There was no Lord Bargrave to speak of.

"This way, if you please."

A footman stretched his hand towards the stone steps, encouraging Lady Juliet and Emma to make their way towards them. One glance toward Juliet's face told Emma that she was in distress, for the girl had gone sheet white and her pale lips were trembling.

Evidently, she had been more concerned about meeting her uncle than she had wanted to admit.

Why does he not come out to greet her?

"Might I ask if Lord Bargrave is at home?"

As she stepped into the townhouse, where an imposing-looking butler awaited them, Emma tried to speak easily and even with a small smile on her lips, but the man's expression remained stoic.

Then after a moment, the butler shook his head.

"No, my Lady. I am afraid that Lord Bargrave has gone out for the afternoon and will not return until much later this evening."

Emma blinked in surprise as a thin slice of anger began to build in her stomach.

"I see."

She did not reach out for Lady Juliet but was afraid of what her charge's reaction would be to such news.

"Everything has been prepared for your arrival, however. The maid will show you to your rooms. If you wish to take tea there, you may do so, otherwise, I shall have it ready in the drawing-room."

Keeping her smile fixed in place, Emma turned to Lady Juliet.

"What would be your preference, my dear? Should you wish to rest for a while in your room?"

Lady Juliet said nothing, turning slightly so that she might face the butler a little more.

"You say that my uncle is gone from the house?"

"Yes, my Lady."

"And when is he expected to return?"

The butler hesitated.

"I... I could not say, my Lady. I believe that he has an evening function to attend also."

"I see." It was with great astonishment that Emma saw the sparkle in Lady Juliet's eyes. She had worried that her charge would be deeply upset over her uncle's absence, but it seemed that the girl was more than delighted. "We shall take tea in the drawing-room. And thereafter, might we explore the house and gardens a little? With my uncle absent I can see no reason for us not to do so."

Emma blinked, but then nodded.

"Yes, I can see no reason to refuse such a request. This is to be your home for the next few months, after all." She glanced at the butler, seeing a line form between his brows. "We shall, of course, make certain to stay away from any private areas and will not enter your uncle's study nor his bedchamber."

"Yes, of course we shall not." Her smile growing steadily, Lady Juliet gestured to the staircase. "And is this the way to our bedchambers?"

"The maid is waiting to show you, my Lady, and the footmen will bring up your trunks shortly."

At that very moment, a small figure hurried towards them, as though she had been waiting for the right moment to reveal herself. Following Lady Juliet, Emma made her way up the staircase, led by the maid. Looking all around her, she took in the townhouse – both its furnishings and its décor. To her mind, it was quite grand indeed – although that assessment might very well come from the fact that her father was only a Baron and she, therefore, had not lived in quite as much comfort as this. A wry smile tugged her mouth and Emma shook her head to herself.

"And this is your room, my Lady."

The maid stepped to one side and pushed open the door as Lady Juliet walked in. The audible gasp echoed back towards Emma, who smiled softly to herself. *At least in this, Lady Juliet is happy.*

"Oh, it is quite lovely. I shall be very happy here, I am sure." Lady Juliet's voice floated back towards her in the air. "Miss Lawder? Where are you?"

"I am here." Walking into the bedchamber, Emma smiled at her charge. "It is good to see you looking a little more cheerful."

"That is because I am in a beautiful house in a beautiful room. My uncle certainly does live in comfort!"

Emma laughed.

"I should expect so, given that he is an Earl."

"Might I show you to your room?"

The maid darted a glance towards Emma, then dropped her head.

"But of course. You have duties you must get to. I quite understand."

"I shall come with you. I would very much like to see your room... if you do not mind, that is?"

Shaking her head, Emma held out one hand towards Lady Juliet.

"I do not mind in the least."

For whatever reason, the maid hesitated. Her eyes went first to Lady Juliet, then to Emma, then down to the floor.

"My room?"

The maid coughed, nodded, and then turned from the room. Emma followed her without hesitation, once more, taking in the decoration and the furnishings. The house appeared to be warm and comfortable, and Emma was certain that Lady Juliet would be happy residing here.

"Wherever are we going? It seems as though we are at the very back of the house!"

Lady Juliet's exclamation made Emma realize that they had been walking through the townhouse in all manner of directions. Outwardly, it had not appeared to be overly large, but now that she was inside, there seemed to be so many little rooms that she was quite lost.

"I shall never be able to find you again!" Emma laughed, ignoring the slight curl of worry in her stomach. "Wherever has Lord Bargrave put me?"

The maid glanced over her shoulder, her lip caught between her teeth. Eventually, she came to a stop. This particular hallway was dim and dark, and the room which Emma stepped into was much the same. There was only one small window and the light it tried to let in was blocked by a large tree branch covered in leaves. It was rather cold, given that very little sunshine could come in, and so very small that it seemed as though the tiny bed could barely fit inside it.

"This is ridiculous! You cannot stay here." Lady Juliet grabbed the maid's arm, pulling the girl back a little. "This cannot be right. Are you attempting to show my companion that she is not welcome here? Bring her to the right bedchamber at once."

The maid's eyes widened and then she dropped her head, so that her chin practically rested on her chest.

"Desist, my dear." It was clear to Emma that the maid was only following orders. "This must be where Lord Bargrave has decided to place me. You need not blame the servants, who are no doubt simply doing as they have been told to."

The maid said nothing, and her head remained low.

"This is ridiculous! You are my companion and a lady in your own right. Why should my uncle put you in such a bedchamber as this? It is small, dank, and dark! There must be many other rooms in this townhouse. I cannot understand his reasons for doing so."

"Nor can I, but we must abide by them." Emma lifted her chin even as her heart began to sink lower. "I am sure I shall be perfectly content."

This room is oppressive, but I must not allow Lady Juliet to see how it affects me. I do not wish to make a poor impression on Lord Bargrave.

"I shall absolutely not permit it!" Lady Juliet tossed her head sharply. "I am not a young lady inclined towards silence when there has been clear inconsideration. I will speak to my uncle at once. Do not unpack any of your things."

Emma laid a calming hand on Lady Juliet's arm.

"You forget that your uncle is absent this evening. I do not think that we will meet him until the morrow."

Lady Juliet's blue eyes narrowed.

"Then *I* shall have another room prepared at once."

A jolt of fear tugged at Emma's heart.

"No, Lady Juliet, you cannot."

"I certainly can, and I shall. I am his niece and I expect both myself and my companion to be treated fairly. To have you reside in here is tantamount to giving you the place of a servant! I am aware that you are my companion, and you are also meant to give me both advice and guidance, but you are a lady born, and in this, I am quite determined, and I will not be swayed." Before Emma could protest or say anything further, Lady Juliet had gestured to the maid, snapping out instructions one after the other. "Send the housekeeper to my rooms. Tell the footman to remove my companion's luggage from this room. And have tea sent to my rooms also. At once, girl, at once!"

Emma held herself back, resisting the urge to counteract everything that Lady Juliet had said. If she were honest, she did not wish to reside here. Everything Lady Juliet had said about the room was true, and it certainly did not fit her standing as a companion. She would not need the best room, and nor would she expect such a room, but to be given something that perhaps a governess, or less, might be offered was more than a little upsetting. After all, she would be amongst society, would dine with Lord Bargrave and Lady Juliet and would attend every society function that Lady Juliet wished. Why then was she being treated with such disregard?

"Come, Miss Lawder." Lady Juliet's voice rang out along the corridor and Emma rubbed one hand over her eyes, uncertain as to what she ought to do. "Do hurry, Miss Lawder. We shall have you settled in your new room within the hour."

Biting her lip, Emma took in a deep breath and then followed her charge. Perhaps this was for the best. The thought of spending months residing in such a dark and dank bedchamber was a distressing one, and as Emma closed the door, she felt a tug of relief nudge at her heart. She could not understand Lord Bargrave's reasons for setting her in such a room, but perhaps Lady Juliet was right to be so insistent. The gentleman clearly needed to be reminded of Emma's standing and this would be one way to do such a thing.

I have been so determined to make the very best of impressions upon Lord Bargrave, but now I fear that we will make a very poor one indeed... although my first thought of his character is a very negative one indeed! Her lips twisted as she continued to follow Lady Juliet back through the house, towards the lady's bedchamber. *I have no joy in the thought of meeting him. I can only pray that he will treat Lady Juliet with more consideration than he has me.*

CHAPTER TWO

Giles scowled, threaded his fingers into his hair, and dropped his elbows onto the large, polished desk in front of him. Having forced himself to rise about an hour earlier, he had not yet broken his fast but had chosen instead to come to the study to look through his correspondence. In the depths of his heart, he knew that this was something which he was doing simply to avoid meeting his niece and her companion, but as yet, it appeared to be working. There was a great deal of correspondence, and should he decide to respond to everybody who had written to him, then he could be in his study for a good part of the day.

And then all that is required is to sit to dinner before we take our leave for the evening.

Having behaved entirely selfishly the previous evening, Giles now found himself with a painful headache and a severe weight of guilt resting upon his heart. Yes, he knew that he ought to have remained at home to greet his niece and her companion, but he had been quite unwilling to give up the dinner invitation which Lady Waterston had offered him. It had been an intimate dinner and he had enjoyed her company, although he would have much preferred if the other two gentlemen and ladies had been absent.

Lord Waterston was not yet back from the continent, and Lady Waterston had declared on more than one occasion just how much she was missing fine company. The spark in her eye and the knowing smile had left him with no question about what it was that she wanted from him, but as yet, he was not willing to give it. From what he knew of the lady, Giles was concerned that any affection shared between them would not be kept solely between themselves - and he had also heard that the lady was somewhat clinging. It had been an enjoyable evening, but certainly not one that he wanted to continue any further.

A tap at the door alerted him to the butler's presence and with a heavy sigh, he lifted his attention from his correspondence.

"Yes?"

Much to his astonishment, it was not the butler who stepped into the room. Rather, there appeared a young lady, with blonde hair pulled back into a delicate chignon and piercing blue eyes which fixed themselves straight to his.

"Uncle." Following a quick curtsey, she walked directly into the room, leaving the door to close behind her. "I thought it best to come and greet you directly, as I am aware that you are very busy this morning. Your butler told me that we could not expect to see you before dinner, but I was not willing to wait that long."

She did not smile, and for whatever reason, Giles found himself a little concerned about her presence. For the first time, he realized that his niece would be corresponding with her mother and father, and would report his behavior to them directly. If he failed in his duties, having already offered to take his niece on, then there might well be hard words from his sister - and surely she had suffered injury enough already, with the ill health of her husband.

"Good morning, Juliet." Rising from his chair, Giles went around the desk to greet his niece. "I am sorry that I was unable to be present yesterday. I had a pressing engagement which could not be missed."

Juliet's blue eyes flickered.

"There must have been a great importance to this dinner and the ball thereafter, Uncle, since it took precedence over my arrival." A slightly cool smile pulled at her lips. "You can imagine my disappointment." Giles harrumphed quietly, having never expected to hear such a thing from his niece. Even though he had never met his niece, Giles had always believed her to be a quiet sort of girl and had not thought that he would hear such determined words from her. "We had a comfortable evening and night, however." Juliet lifted her chin, never once shifting her gaze from his face. "I should inform you that I have moved my companion from the bedchamber *you* had designated for her to one that is much more suitable."

Giles blinked.

"I beg your pardon?"

"I have removed her from the bedchamber which was set aside for her and placed her in a room closer to my own. You are aware, Uncle, that she is a companion and not a governess? Not a lady's maid?" Astonishment tied a knot in his tongue. "The bedchamber was most unsuitable. She is the daughter of a Baron and should be treated as such, do you not think?"

"I do not believe that I have been considering her in any other way."

A cold hand tightened around his neck at the cool smile which spread across his niece's face.

"Then why, might I ask, did you place her in such a dingy bedchamber, when there are plenty of perfectly suitable bedchambers available in your house?" Lady Juliet's hands went to her hips, and one eyebrow arched questioningly. Rather than have an answer ready for her, Giles found himself quite astonished. He was not angry nor upset, but rather utterly amazed that this slip of a girl thought she could speak to him in such a manner. Worse, that she could step into his house and undermine his authority in such a way! "I believe that Mama has made it perfectly clear to you just how much Miss Lawder means to us." Before he could even begin to form an answer, Lady Juliet was speaking again, perhaps seeing a flicker of anger in his eyes. "Her father thinks very little of her. She is considered nothing more than a burden to him, even though, by rights, she ought to be a lady in amongst society as I am. She arrived with us very soon after father became ill. Mother thought that I might gain relief and companionship during what was a terribly difficult time, but Miss Lawder has brought both Mother, and myself, a great deal of comfort." Lady Juliet shook her head and sighed, finally dropping her gaze from his. "Did you know that her father, Baron Wakefield, has made certain that any money she makes is sent directly to him? I do not think that Miss Lawder has a penny of her own and, of course, she can do nothing about it, for it is her father's prerogative to do as he sees fit. For someone who has been treated so cruelly by her own flesh and blood, I think that we must do that we can, to show her as much generosity as possible. As I have just stated, she has become very dear to both myself and my mother in such a short while."

Giles drew in a deep breath, his emotions all of a confusion.

"You are certainly rather forthright, Lady Juliet."

And most able to make me feel very guilty indeed over my choice of bedchamber for the lady which, in itself, is a very small thing indeed.

A hint of a smile danced around Lady Juliet's lips.

"I believe that I am much like my mother, Uncle."

Despite his frustration, a laugh escaped from the corner of his mouth.

"In that I believe you are quite right, Lady Juliet. My sister was always stubborn and determined, and it appears that you may also have that trait. I do not know how your father survives with both of you in his house!"

Lady Juliet's smile lingered.

"I believe that my father would prefer me to be forthright and blunt, rather than shy and retiring."

I cannot imagine why.

"You have made your point quite clearly. I confess that I did not think of Miss Lawder's social standing when I gave her that bedchamber."

Seeing his niece's eyebrows lift, he spread his hands and shrugged, thinking that would be enough of an explanation.

"You sought to keep her from society rather than encourage her to join with it. And that even before you were introduced to her."

Guilt reared its ugly head in Giles' heart, but he ignored it with an effort. Shrugging, he turned away from his niece and picked up his brandy glass, which was unfortunately empty.

"You forget, Lady Juliet, that I have no knowledge of companions. I have no experience with such creatures either. I was only doing as I thought best."

A small yet triumphant smile caught the edge of Lady Juliet's mouth.

"I quite understand, Uncle. I am glad that you are willing to accept the change in circumstances."

It is not as though I have any opportunity to refuse it.

"Indeed." Forcing a smile, Giles gestured to the door. "As you yourself have said, I am very busy this morning. I fear I shall not see you again until we dine this evening."

Much to his frustration, however, Lady Juliet did not move.

"And is there any entertainment for us this evening? Or are you again to go into society without us?"

This is going to be more difficult than I had anticipated.

"I have nothing planned for this evening as I was certain you would both require some time to rest and recover after your long journey to London."

"How very considerate." Lady Juliet's smile was a little fierce. "Then tomorrow, I assume? I am very much looking forward to entering society. You do recall that I am to be presented tomorrow afternoon?"

His mind spinning frantically, Giles gave her a swift nod.

"Yes, tomorrow afternoon, of course. Thereafter, there are many things I have planned for you and for your companion."

This was of course a complete mistruth, for Giles had no invitations secured, nor had he made any plans of his own.

"I am delighted to hear it." With a smile, Lady Juliet finally turned towards the door, leaving Giles to breathe out a sigh of relief. "I shall inform Miss Lawder at once. You have not met her as yet, have you?"

Giles shook his head.

"No, that pleasure is still to come, and shall happen this evening."

Lady Juliet smiled and left him without another word. Giles dropped his head forward, letting out a sigh of frustration as he did so.

Now I must find some sort of entertainment for my niece and her companion for tomorrow night.

For whatever reason, it had not occurred to him that his niece would require company and entertainment upon her arrival to London, although he had, at the very least, remembered that she was to be presented. He had spoken of her presence in London to no-one, perhaps out of a mistaken hope that the situation might never take place. In the back of his mind had been the prayer that Lady Juliet's father would recover in time for them all come to London.

"It appears that I have been a little foolish."

Straightening, Giles turned back to his desk, continuing to mutter to himself. Picking up his quill, he found that no inspiration came to him as he prepared to continue with his correspondence. His thoughts were centered solely on his niece. The last thing he had expected was to see her so fiery and filled with determination. And yet, that stubborn trait was a part of his family, and now that he thought of it, had he not seen it in his own sister many years ago?

Her companion will have much to do to improve her. Lady Juliet must be shown how to behave and speak appropriately in society. Dropping his quill, Giles went in search of his empty brandy glass. The Season stretched out in front of him, no longer filled with joys and delights, but rather with struggle and strain. He was not to have the enjoyment he had relished for so many years. Instead, there was responsibility and burden and Giles wished with every fiber of his being that he had never agreed to sponsor his niece into society in the first place.

"Good evening, Uncle."

Choosing to remain unsmiling, Giles rose from his chair.

"Good evening. It is good of you to finally join me for dinner." With a lifted eyebrow, he gestured to the empty chair at the other end of the table. "It has been at least five minutes since the dinner gong sounded."

"Thank you for your patience." Juliet's smile was sweet but there was no brightness in her eyes. "I confess that I was a little tardy due to a slight tear in my gown. Miss Lawder was quick to fix it, however, so we are only a few minutes late." Giles nodded, his smile tight, as tension began to flood the space between them. They had only been in each other's company for a very short while, and yet it seemed that this unsettling feeling only grew with every meeting. *Perhaps I have upset her by being so inconsiderate – in her eyes – towards her companion!* "You have not yet been introduced to Miss Lawder."

"No, indeed I have not."

Finally pulling his attention away from Lady Juliet, Giles looked to the young lady standing behind his niece.

"Uncle, this is Miss Emma Lawder. Miss Lawder, this is my uncle, the Earl of Bargrave." Lady Juliet smiled. "I should also have informed you that Miss Lawder is the daughter of Baron Wakefield."

A slightly knowing smile crept into her eyes as she studied him, sending another stab of guilt into Giles' heat.

"Good evening, Miss Lawder." As the lady stepped into

the candlelight a little more, Giles blinked in surprise. This was not the picture he had formed in his mind of his niece's companion. He had thought that she would have been a good deal older, and perhaps even a slightly wrinkled creature with much of life behind her. He had assumed that her father had sent her to be a companion due to her age – but this willowy young lady could only be, at most, a few years older than Lady Juliet! Clearing his throat, Giles dropped into a bow. "I am very glad to meet you."

"Good evening, Lord Bargrave." The brown-haired young lady smiled softly and dropped into an elegant curtsey. "I know that Lady Juliet is glad indeed to be in London at long last. I will, of course, do all that I can to support her as she traverses society with your guidance and patronage. I thank you also for your generosity in permitting me to reside here for the Season, in what is such a lovely house."

Giles did not miss the way Juliet's eyes lit up at this remark.

Was that particular comment meant to be a comment on the bedchamber I first gave her?

Shrugging inwardly, he returned to his chair, thinking that it would be best to leave the conversation where it was at present.

"Come now, the food will be getting cold if we do not sit to eat together."

Waiting for the ladies to take their seats, he snapped his fingers before sitting down himself and, within seconds, the foot was served.

"It is very exciting that Lady Juliet will be presented tomorrow."

Giles cleared his throat.

"Yes, indeed, most exciting."

Another glance towards the companion told him that

she and Lady Juliet were sharing a secret smile. Had they already planned what they were to converse about? Was there to be an attempt to pile guilt upon his shoulders?

"What is it that you have planned for Lady Juliet tomorrow evening, might I ask?"

Miss Lawder sent a warm smile in Giles' direction, but it only caused his brows to lower all the more.

This is my niece's doing. She does not believe that I have made any plans for her whatsoever.

"You need not concern yourself with my intentions for Lady Juliet, Miss Lawder. I am more than capable." The smile on Miss Lawder's face quickly dropped, and Giles looked away, clearing his throat for what was the second time. "I shall inform you tomorrow, Lady Juliet, about what we are to attend and when we are leaving. I will make sure to give you enough time to prepare."

Lady Juliet's eyes narrowed slightly as she looked straight at him, her fork clasped in one hand.

"Miss Lawder was only asking, Uncle. And as my companion, it is her role to be present at most events which I attend, to chaperone me when you are not immediately available. Is there any need for such secrecy?"

"I am not being secretive in the slightest. I simply do not need to be questioned as to whether or not I am able to care for my niece."

Miss Lawder blinked rapidly and for a moment, and Giles thought that she would drop her head and press a napkin to her eyes. It was not his intention to upset her, of course, but rather that he wanted to make it quite plain that he was able to take care of his niece and her requirements without any additional support from a companion. Then Miss Lawder lifted her head.

"You mistake my intentions, Lord Bargrave. I am not

questioning you, nor am I in anyway suggesting that you are inadequate. Quite frankly, my Lord, I am a little surprised at such a reaction."

Her eyes were clear as they met his for a long moment, leaving Giles without an answer.

I have reacted badly to the lady, simply because of my niece. His conscience pricked him, and he opened his mouth to apologize, only for Lady Juliet to begin a conversation with her companion which excluded him entirely. Grimacing, Giles picked up his fork and began to eat. His relationship with his niece was going to be more difficult to navigate than he had expected, and now he had the companion to deal with also.

I have two feisty, forthright young ladies residing under my roof. His scowl grew as he jabbed his fork into the meat on his plate. *This, I fear, will be one of the least enjoyable Seasons that I have ever known… and it is all my own fault.*

CHAPTER THREE

"You did very well, my dear."

"Thank you."

Lady Juliet seemed to glow with an effervescent spirit as she joined Emma at the bottom of the stairs.

"I am sure that your uncle was very pleased with you."

Lady Juliet snorted and rolled her eyes in a most unladylike fashion.

"Unfortunately, my uncle was busy talking to another lady rather than paying attention to me as I was presented to the Queen."

"Oh." Emma's consideration of Lord Bargrave dropped still further as she looked towards the top of the stairs, seeing him in deep conversation with a lady she did not know. "I am sure that he has something wonderful planned for you this evening. He does not understand the significance of this moment, that is all."

Lady Juliet laughed and shook her head.

"You are to think the best of him, I see. I, however, will not be so easily taken in. I think that my uncle is quite a selfish fellow, unused to having to give anything of himself to anyone."

"That may be so, but I am sure he will do the very best for you."

Looping her arm through Emma's, Lady Juliet let out a long sigh.

"You say such things even though he spoke to you most unfairly last evening. That is very gracious of you." Emma licked her lips but did not respond. Lord Bargrave's reaction to what had been a simple question had been entirely unexpected and had unsettled her a great deal. She had seen in his response a slight fear that he would fail his niece and, while she had been surprised and upset by his reaction, Emma had chosen not to hold it against him. "I do not know my uncle particularly well as yet, but I am certain that this season will reveal the true depths of his character."

"I am quite certain that he cares about you. Whatever this evening is to bring, it will be most enjoyable, I am sure."

Smiling warmly, Emma cast a glance back over her shoulder, her eyes swiftly catching Lord Bargrave's. He was descending the stairs, coming after them with long strides as a slight frown pulled at his brow.

If he would only smile, then I am quite sure that he would be much more handsome.

The thought charged around her mind, making Emma smile to herself as she turned her attention back to her charge.

It was not that she considered Lord Bargrave to be unhandsome, but rather that his seemingly permanent dark frown did nothing to lift his expression. She had not even seen him smile as yet!

"Miss Lawder, Lady Juliet." Lord Bargrave's deep voice

caught their attention and Emma turned her head to look in his direction. "Wait a moment if you will."

"But of course, Uncle." Lady Juliet stepped to one side, turning slightly so that she could wait for her uncle to join them. "I do hope that we did not pull you away from your conversation with...?"

Lord Bargrave's frown etched itself all the more deeply across his forehead.

"Lady Peterson – and no, you did not. I was merely confirming the details with her for this evening's gathering."

Emma looked up in surprise, although it was Lady Juliet who spoke first.

"This evening's gathering?"

"Lord and Lady Peterson are giving a Ball this evening, in light of their daughter's presentation to the Queen. We are all cordially invited."

Casting a glance towards Lady Juliet, Emma silently begged her to express gratitude towards her uncle for such a thing.

"I see." Lady Juliet's tone was a little cool. "We are to attend the ball thrown in another young lady's honor? We go as her guests?"

"Yes." Lord Bargrave did not seem to find any difficulty in such a situation, for the line in his forehead lessoned somewhat. "Miss Matterson will be the main focus of the evening, of course, but that does not mean that other young ladies such as yourself cannot make their come out also. Lady Peterson was most eager for you to attend - I believe that she hopes that you and her daughter may become good friends."

Seeing the way that Lady Juliet's frown deepened, and how she opened her mouth to send a sharp retort to her uncle, Emma shook her head swiftly, managing to catch her charge's eye. Lady Juliet's lips bunched to one side, and she looked away, but much to Emma's relief, remained silent.

"That sounds like an excellent endeavor, my Lord." Sending a quick smile in Lord Bargrave's direction, Emma stepped forward and slipped her hand through Lady Juliet's arm. "Come Lady Juliet, we should return to the carriage. There is much to prepare for this evening." Her charge stepped forward at once, although her head was low and her eyes a little dull. Emma knew precisely why Lady Juliet was so very upset, but chose not to say anything about it. It was not the wisest consideration to take a young woman to another young lady's ball, but Lord Bargrave was clearly doing what he thought was best. "Have you decided what gown you will wear?" Keeping her voice light, Emma walked Lady Juliet back towards the entrance. "You have many beautiful gowns, but I am certain that you told me of one in particular which was to be used for your first venture into society." A small sniff came from Lady Juliet in lieu of an answer. "You will have an excellent evening, I am sure," Emma continued dropping her voice just a little so that Lord Bargrave would not overhear. "Pray do not concern yourself so, Lady Juliet. It will all go marvelously well, I am certain."

Arriving at the carriage, Emma waited for Lady Juliet to climb inside before following suit. Before she could do so, however, a heavy hand settled on her shoulder, forcing her attention towards Lord Bargrave.

"I have upset my niece, I think." Lord Bargrave was not looking at her, and Emma too dropped her gaze, uncertain as to how to answer him. "Is what I have organized not sufficient?"

The barking manner in which he spoke to her did not encourage Emma to tell him the truth.

"It is sufficient, my Lord." Speaking somewhat stiffly, Emma looked towards the carriage. "We will need to return to the house at once, Lord Bargrave. Lady Juliet requires time to prepare for this evening."

Lord Bargrave coughed and shook his head.

"Why do I have the impression that you are not being entirely honest with me?"

"If you will excuse me."

Choosing not to answer him, Emma stepped away and walked directly to the carriage, climbing the steps so that she might sit next to Lady Juliet. Lord Bargrave was the most confusing gentleman. He had not made clear preparations for his niece and then seemed a little upset when she did not react with as much gladness as he'd expected.

Perhaps I was wrong not to answer him, but I cannot tell him anything other than the truth and that, I fear, may cause trouble we don't need!

"My uncle is not going to join us, it seems."

Lady Juliet's expression was a little pinched.

"No?" Glancing out of the carriage window she saw Lord Bargrave wave the carriage into motion, then turned and strode directly away from them. "Perhaps that is for the best." Settling back in her seat, Emma tried to smile as warmly as she could towards her charge. "A ball this evening. How wonderful!"

Lady Juliet shook her head, her eyes suddenly glistening with unshed tears.

"We are to attend a ball which is being given for another young lady, who is also just making her come out. It is as we both believed: my uncle has given very little consideration to my situation here. It is not as though such a ball is unwelcome, but rather that all of the attention will be on Miss Matterson. Every gentleman will be looking at her, seeking *her* attention. There will be very little left for the rest of us."

Reaching across, Emma grasped Lady Juliet's hand.

"You will gain much attention, I am sure. You may be quite correct in your consideration of your uncle, but we must make the best of it. Allow yourself to be a little excited about the prospect of your first ball, my dear. It will be a very grand event indeed, and not one easily forgotten!"

A tiny smile lifted the edge of Lady Juliet's mouth, and the sheen of tears in her eyes began to fade.

"Thank you, Miss Lawder. You are most encouraging."

"I am glad you find me so. I am aware that you have a great many hopes and expectations for your first Season and, whilst not all of them will be fulfilled, I will do all that I can to encourage you and support you throughout everything that happens during these next few weeks." She smiled, tilting her head as she released Lady Juliet's hand. "So, we must now turn our thoughts to your gown and what you are to have adorning your hair. We have some time before we must depart for the ball - and I have every intention of making certain that you are the most beautiful young lady in all of London this evening."

This brought a warm smile to Lady Juliet's face.

"Thank you, Miss Lawder... or may I now call you Emma? We have been so very formal these last few months, but now I feel as though we are becoming great friends and such formality seems quite out of place."

"Of course." Her heart lifting, Emma looked out of the carriage window, seeing London pass by. "I am quite sure that this evening will be everything you hoped for, Juliet. Everything and maybe even more."

"Is my niece downstairs yet?"

Emma turned just as Lord Bargrave walked into the drawing-room. Dropping into an awkward curtsey, she took a moment to answer, gathering herself.

"She will be down momentarily, my Lord."

The gentleman harrumphed, and Emma did not know where to look, finding the tension between them suddenly growing into a great and ominous presence.

I do not know him particularly well as yet. I cannot make any judgments about his character. That would not be fair.

"I believe that you think me a little unfeeling."

Emma's eyes shot to his.

"Unfeeling, my Lord?"

"You think that I have done poorly as regards my niece."

Rather than choosing to answer in the affirmative or the negative, Emma simply spread her hands.

"Why does it matter, my Lord, what my opinion is? I am only a companion - you are her uncle. You will do as you see fit and as you believe is best."

This answer did not seem to find favor with him, for Lord Bargrave's frown grew and the familiar line drew itself between his eyebrows once more. Emma did not shrink from him, however. She allowed her gaze to rest on his features, taking in his heavy eyebrows, the way his fair hair flopped over his forehead and the intensity of his eyes as he studied her. In the candlelight, she could not quite make out the color of them, but if there was a family trait, then she expected them to be blue, just as Lady Juliet's were. All in all, Emma would certainly consider Lord Bargrave to be a handsome gentleman, albeit with that continual heavy frown lingering across his forehead.

"You are scrutinizing me heavily, Miss Lawder."

The heat of embarrassment rose in her chest. She had not realized that her study of him had been so obvious, nor that he had been watching her.

"I do not mean to do so, my Lord. Forgive me." She did not lower her gaze entirely, however, wanting to give a reason for her consideration of him so that he would not think her a strange creature. "It is only that I sought out family similarities between your features and those of Lady Juliet."

"And did you find any?"

Much to Emma's astonishment, the corner of Lord Bargrave's lips quirked upwards and the heat of embarrassment in her belly suddenly changed to a strange fluttering. This was the first time that she had ever seen even a hint of joviality on his face. It changed his features entirely, for his eyes suddenly sparkled and his brows suddenly lifted from their usual heavy position.

"I... I believe that I have, yes, although I find myself wondering whether or not your eyes are of a similar color to Lady Juliet's."

Why am I saying such things? I need not give any further explanation.

"My eyes are blue, in fact." Lord Bargrave smiled suddenly, and Emma's breath caught in her chest. "They have a hint of green here and there – a gift from my father, I believe, but on the whole, they remain mostly blue." His smile began to fade, and his eyebrows lowered to their usual position. "You say that my niece also has blue eyes? I confess that I have not noticed."

Emma nodded.

"Yes, she does."

Again, her eyes were drawn towards Lord Bargrave, and she found herself unable to pull her gaze away. She had not seen this side of him before. She had not even seen him smile before, but that tiny crook of his mouth changed his expression so drastically that she could barely keep her astonishment hidden.

"I do not know my niece." Lord Bargrave put both hands behind his back but did not allow his gaze to linger on her. "I will admit to you, Miss Lawder, that I am a little surprised at her... fierceness. I ought not to be, of course, for, as a child, my sister displayed the very same strength."

"Might I ask what your expectation was of your niece?"

Lord Bargrave shrugged.

"I expected a quiet, genteel young lady who would do as she was asked and would not, for example, move her companion from one bedchamber to another without so much as a by-your-leave!"

A slight flush caught Emma's cheeks and she once more dropped her gaze. There was nothing for her to say in response to such a remark for, as yet, she could not be sure of whether or not Lord Bargrave saw any mistake in his decision to place her where he had – and it was certainly not her place to state such a thing directly!

"You will have to make sure that she traverses society with great care, Miss Lawder."

Her head lifted.

"Yes, my Lord, of course."

"She cannot be allowed to speak with such forthrightness in company. Her sole purpose is to find a suitable match, is it not? And no gentleman of the *ton* will wish for her company if they find her to be as outspoken as I do."

Turning away from her, he marched towards the

window as though such a statement ought to be accepted without question, as though he thought she would simply agree with him.

Emma's heart twisted and every good consideration of Lord Bargrave which had filled her mind these last few moments shattered completely.

"You would have your niece pretend to be someone she is not?"

Lord Bargrave's head spun back towards her.

"I beg your pardon?"

"You are asking me to encourage your niece to pretend that she is not as she truly is. You think it best that she hide her true character, that she play herself false, so that the gentlemen of the *ton* might think well of her."

"I see no difficulty in that."

Emma shook her head, her hands going to her hips.

"Then pray tell me Lord Bargrave, what would happen should Lady Juliet marry? Her husband will not know the true Lady Juliet, he will be making his vows to a woman he does not truly know. And Lady Juliet will not be able to hide such traits forever - although I do confess that I do not think she would be willing to hide them at all! Such a marriage would be a great burden for both husband and wife. It would lead to only difficulty, strife, and pain."

Lord Bargrave's lip curled, and his eyes narrowed slightly.

"And you speak from experience, do you?"

Emma lifted her chin, refusing to allow the slight to injure her.

"I speak from the very same position as you, Lord Bargrave. I will *not* encourage Lady Juliet to behave in such a way. It is my belief that she must remain true to herself and not shrink back simply so that the gentlemen of the *ton* might think well of her."

Lord Bargrave's eyes narrowed still further.

"Then I fear you doom her to a life of spinsterhood."

"And I am quite of the opposite opinion." Aware that her voice was rising, Emma dropped her hands and took a steadying breath. "It is my belief that there will be many gentlemen in society who will see Lady Juliet's character and think it beautiful."

The gentleman let out a huff of breath, closed his eyes, and shook his head.

"It is just as well that *I* am her sponsor into society, and you are only her companion. This is the path I shall be leading my niece. It would make things a great deal easier if you would simply align your approach with mine."

"I shall not." Emma lifted her chin, unafraid. "I am her companion and her friend. I shall always do what I believe is best for her."

"And you shall find, Uncle, that I am not so easily biddable." Turning, Emma saw Lady Juliet walking into the drawing-room. From the sparks flashing in her eyes, it appeared that she had been listening to the conversation for the last few minutes. "My mother has always encouraged me to stay true to myself. My father has wished me to be a strong young woman who is not afraid to express opinions. I should do them both a dishonor if I behaved in any other way."

Lord Bargrave scowled.

"Things are very different here in London, Lady Juliet."

"That may be so, but you will find me less than willing to do as you have suggested." Coming to stand next to Emma, Lady Juliet looped one arm through hers. "Now, are we to go to the ball? The last thing I want is for us to be tardy to what is my very first social occasion!"

Lord Bargrave's expression was so dark that, for a moment, Emma believed he was about to turn around and cancel their engagement completely. He turned away, his shoulders hunched and his back stiff and straight. Swallowing hard, Emma glanced towards Lady Juliet, who appeared quite calm, looking towards her uncle and waiting in expectant silence.

"Make your way to the carriage." Lord Bargrave's voice was gruff, and he flung out a hand towards them without turning around. "I shall join you in a few minutes."

Emma did not need to be given another opportunity. Releasing Lady Juliet's arm she hurried to the door, with Lady Juliet walking swiftly behind her.

"I thank you for your courage." Lady Juliet whispered into Emma's ear as they made their way to the front of the house. "I am very grateful to you for your responses to my uncle. You are right. I am entirely unwilling to pretend. If any gentleman is to consider me, then they must know my true character. I could not be deceitful."

"And I should never encourage you to be."

Stepping back so that Lady Juliet could climb into the carriage, Emma cast a quick glance up towards the drawing room window. Was it just her imagination, or was Lord Bargrave still standing by the window?

I do not know what he thinks of me now, but I must be honest with both myself and with him.

Her heart dropped to the ground as she considered the next few months living under his roof, fearing that it would not be a pleasant atmosphere. But then she recalled the way that his lips had quirked, and his expression had changed so dramatically. Was there any chance that she might see that side of him again? Or would he remain as he always had been thus far – frowning upon every single thing that either she or Lady Juliet did, and making it quite clear that he considered their presence in his house a burden.

As much as she might hope for the former, Emma was convinced it would be the latter... and that would make her stay in London very trying indeed.

CHAPTER FOUR

"Pray tell me who is this young lady?"

Giles coughed harshly, disliking the fact that his friend was looking with such interest toward his niece.

"*That* would be my niece."

Lord Kincaid wiggled his eyebrows in a most disconcerting manner.

"And are you looking for a husband for her?"

"If I was, I certainly would not recommend you."

Laughing, Lord Kincaid elbowed Giles a little too hard.

"Come now, you cannot think me so terrible! You certainly cannot refuse to introduce me. Your niece will require many introductions to gentlemen if she is to be known in society - and I am only too happy to oblige."

Giles let out a long slow breath, his eyes a little narrowed as he looked towards his friend.

"We shall not remain friends for long if you do anything to upset her. In fact, I shall have no hesitation in calling you out, should you so much as touch her."

The smile fled from Lord Kincaid's face. Giles kept his

expression stony, meaning dripping from his every word. Before Lord Kincaid could reply, however, Lady Juliet and Miss Lawder came over to join them.

"Is everything quite all right?"

A little irritated at his niece's direct question, Giles forced a smile and turned to face her.

"Lady Juliet, allow me to introduce you to one of my dear friends, the Earl of Kincaid. Kincaid – my niece, Lady Juliet Millwood."

Glancing towards Lord Kincaid, Giles was a little confused at the frown which pulled at his friend's brow. In fact, it took Lord Kincaid a moment or two to respond to the introduction and, much to Giles' surprise, Lord Kincaid's eyes rested solely on Miss Lawder instead of Lady Juliet.

"I am very pleased to make your acquaintance." Dropping into a curtsey, Lady Juliet turned to her companion. "Since my uncle appears to have forgotten about my companion, allow me to introduce her. Lord Kincaid, this is Miss Lawder, daughter to Baron Wakefield."

Lord Kincaid bowed low.

"A pleasure, Miss Lawder. I must hope that, as Lady Juliet's companion, you are also going to be present for dancing and soirees and the like?"

His eyes glittered and Giles' stomach twisted. He knew his friend all too well. Such interest in Miss Lawder was not because he cared for the lady at all, but rather because he was considering what sort of pleasure he might gain from her company. Pleasure which would be fleeting rather than permanent.

"I hardly think –"

"Of course, Miss Lawder is free to do as she wishes!" Lady Juliet exclaimed, interrupting him before he could finish. "If you wish to dance with her, then you must ask her directly." A gentle laugh escaped from her as Miss Lawder dropped her eyes, a blush warming her cheeks. "Although I cannot promise that you will be granted what you ask for."

"My purpose here is to simply accompany Lady Juliet wherever she goes." Miss Lawder lifted her chin and looked directly towards Lord Kincaid, her color still high. "I thank you, however, for your kind consideration."

"But if Lady Juliet commands it, then obey her, you must!" Lord Kincaid grinned as Lady Juliet laughed softly. "Perhaps I shall still have a dance from you one day soon, Miss Lawder!"

Giles cleared his throat.

"Now, as I was saying –"

"I am quite sure that I am much too late to ask, but if you have space on your dance card, I should be very grateful for the opportunity to dance with you, Lady Juliet."

Before Giles could protest, Lady Juliet smiled and slipped her dance card from her wrist, handing it to Lord Kincaid without a word.

"How wonderful." Bending his head so that he might look at the dance card, Lord Kincaid took a few moments before signing his name. "The country dance. One of my favorites."

"Is it indeed?" Lady Juliet smiled, and Giles' stomach dropped. "The country dance is also one of my favorites, Lord Kincaid. How very fortunate."

Lord Kincaid grinned.

"I look forward to dancing it all the more, then."

As he went to open his mouth to interrupt the conversation, Giles was prevented from doing so by the arrival of another gentleman. A few moments later, Lady Juliet was making her way towards the center of the room, ready to dance the quadrille, whilst Miss Lawder stood quietly to one side, watching her charge carefully. Giles turned his attention back to Lord Kincaid.

"You have understood me plainly, I hope."

Lord Kincaid held up both hands, palm outwards.

"Yes indeed, you need not reiterate it. I will show the greatest care towards your niece, although...." Giles watched as Lord Kincaid's eyes shifted towards Miss Lawder. "You must understand that it was not your niece who first caught my attention. Lady Juliet is very lovely indeed, of course, but I confess that my attention was turning towards Miss Lawder at the first."

Miss Lawder?

"She is also of an eligible age, is she not?"

"I believe so, but she is my niece's companion."

Lord Kincaid chuckled.

"That makes things all the easier, does it not? A companion is not looking for matrimony - they cannot, given their position. However, they may well be interested in a little... flirtation." His eyes glinted, but Giles felt his jaw tighten in response.

"You will find that Miss Lawder is not that way inclined."

"And you know this for certain?" Lord Kincaid waggled his eyebrows and Giles curled one hand into a fist in an attempt to keep hold of his temper. "Can it be that you have already attempted to persuade her towards you?"

Beginning now to wonder what he had ever seen in friendship with Lord Kincaid, Giles shook his head sharply.

"Good heavens, no. I fear I am more of a gentleman than you believe me to be."

A choking laugh came from Lord Kincaid.

"I hardly think that can be true! Have you forgotten the last few Seasons? You must know that I'm all too aware of the many dalliances you have enjoyed... and I am certain that one of them at least was a companion."

"I am quite sure that I have never once laid a finger on a companion. I may have enjoyed the company of many fine ladies, but I would never injure an innocent young lady. I would never ruin their prospects nor their reputation simply for my own pleasures." Speaking with great determination, Giles narrowed his eyes slightly, fixing them to Lord Kincaid. "Whether or not you have the same standards, I will tell you now that you are not to touch Miss Lawder."

"And I do not think that that is your decision to make." Lord Kincaid's smile grew fixed, his eyes a little stony. "She is a paid companion, yes, but she is not in *your* employ."

"She resides in my house."

"But you do not determine her actions. You have no right to do so. That would only come from the father and mother of Lady Juliet, would it not? If I should show an interest in Miss Lawder, then you have no right to prevent it."

Giles' fingernails cut into the soft skin of his palm as he again fought to keep hold of his temper.

"Your interest would only be fleeting."

"Be that as it may, it may be the only interest that the lady ever receives - and she might very well respond with all eagerness. I confess I am a little surprised that you are showing such protectiveness of someone who is only a paid companion. She means nothing to you. Why are you seeking to prevent her from having even the smallest amount of happiness?"

Giles opened his mouth to speak, to give some sort of explanation, but none came. Lord Kincaid snorted his derision, turned on his heel sharply, and walked away, leaving

Giles to stand alone, wondering why he had not been able to find something to say.

His eyes shifted to Miss Lawder, seeing her standing by herself, still watching Lady Juliet. She was entirely unaware of Lord Kincaid's consideration, but given how she had responded to his suggestion that they dance together, Giles was convinced that she would reject any genuine interest from the gentleman. *So why then, am I so perturbed?*

There did not come an easy answer. Thus far, Giles had found Miss Lawder to be a little irritating and, given the fact that she was *not* his responsibility, there was no reason for him to feel such concern. Could he not trust that Miss Lawder had enough sense to ignore Lord Kincaid's interest?

"You are staring at me, my Lord." Without shifting her gaze to his, Miss Lawder spoke quietly, her expression quite calm. "Have I upset you in some way?"

A flush of embarrassment sent heat cascading into Giles' cheeks.

"No, Miss Lawder. Forgive my scrutiny."

Her hazel eyes darted to his and, for just a second, a small smile curved her lips.

"Given that you have forgiven my previous study of you, it seems only fair that I should return the favor." Once more her interest turned towards Lady Juliet. "I am relieved to know that I have not offended you."

For whatever reason, Giles found himself suddenly propelled towards Miss Lawder's side.

"Miss Lawder, I must speak to you about Lord Kincaid," he said quietly.

Blinking, she turned to face him, her eyes a little wide.

"Lord Kincaid?"

"He has expressed an interest in you. I would urge you to stay far from him."

Miss Lawder stared up into his face, color fading from her cheeks. Darkness cast a shadow over her eyes, and she put both hands on her hips, tilting her chin up towards him.

"You think that I might be caught by someone such as Lord Kincaid? Do you truly believe that I would forget my duties so soon?"

"That is not what I meant." Confusion furrowed his brow. "Miss Lawder, I –"

Her hands dropped to her side.

"Then you seek to warn me away from him, because it would be shameful for a companion to capture the affections of a gentleman." Her eyes closed and she turned her head away. "I can assure you, Lord Bargrave, that you need not have any concern. My only thought is of Lady Juliet. I am well aware of my responsibilities to her and to her family." Much to Giles' horror, a sheen of tears had formed in her eyes when she looked back towards him. "I am all too aware of my circumstances. Had my father been willing, I might well have found myself amongst society and been Lady Juliet's friend rather than her companion. But I am grateful for what I have been given. I will not shirk my duties for the sake of my own happiness. You need not have any concern, Lord Bargrave. No gentleman will ever pull me from Lady Juliet's side."

Giles opened his mouth to say something more, just as Lady Juliet walked back towards them.

"Lord Kincaid is an excellent dancer, I must say," said Lady Juliet.

Her eyes flicked from Giles to Miss Lawder and then back again, her smile drifting away.

Seeing the questions growing in her eyes, Giles cleared his throat.

"I am glad to hear it."

"Are you quite all right, Emma?" Lady Juliet put one hand on Miss Lawder's arm. "You appear a little pale."

"I am quite all right." Miss Lawder's gaze flicked up towards Giles for a fraction of a second as a smile attempted to draw itself across her lips. "Should you like to take a turn about the room, Lady Juliet?"

She did not give Lady Juliet any other option but to agree, turning away at once and beginning to make her way around the room. Giles caught the sharp glance Lady Juliet shot him, but he merely shrugged one shoulder and turned away himself. His niece did not need to have any explanation from him for, even if he attempted to give her one, Giles had no doubt that she would make him feel more guilty than he already did.

～

"YOU LOOK A LITTLE PERTURBED, I must say."

Giles rolled his eyes.

"I have a niece residing with me. With her companion. Of course, I am perturbed!"

"Your niece appears to be doing very well!"

Giles forced a smile as Lady Winthrop touched his arm with one delicate hand, squeezing it gently.

"I confess that I have very little experience when it comes to dealing with one's niece. I have never had to put a young lady through her come out before."

Lady Winthrop sent a simpering smile in his direction.

"If you have any need of me, I should be more than happy to help. Perhaps we might discuss your niece and her requirements one evening?"

Taking a deep breath, Giles forced a smile.

"I should be very grateful for any assistance. Lady Winthrop... but alas, it must be only that."

Lady Winthrop moved closer, her hand going to his arm once more.

"Why must it be so? You and I have shared many enjoyable evenings together before, have we not? I cannot understand why we would not be able to resume such a connection now."

"It is solely because I have my niece residing with me, Lady Winthrop." Warmth began to spread up his arm and into his chest as memories of the many enjoyable occasions he had spent in Lady Winthrop's company flooded his mind. "I cannot enjoy the same freedoms I once did."

"That is quite ridiculous. I shall not accept such a reason!"

Lady Winthrop's warm smile sent a flush of heat straight through him.

"You are most persuasive, Lady Winthrop."

Despite his determination not to do so, Giles found his fingers curling around Lady Winthrop's hand. Turning away so that they stood a little more in the shadows at the edge of the ballroom, Giles smiled down into her eyes.

"You will find, Lord Bargrave, that widowed ladies such as myself usually succeed in their intentions."

"Is that so?" Giles chuckled as Lady Winthrop fluttered her eyelashes at him. The problems with his niece and with Miss Lawder suddenly seemed to disappear as he looked down into the familiar smile of Lady Winthrop. The guilt which had assuaged his soul for the last hour suddenly melted away as all thought of Miss Lawder and Lord Kincaid disappeared completely. "Perhaps I can be convinced after all, Lady Winthrop."

"I am very glad to hear it. Shall we say tomorrow evening?"

Giles was about to answer in the affirmative when a sudden movement caught his eye. Miss Lawder was standing to his left, her eyes fixed straight ahead as Lady Juliet continued to dance what was her fifth dance of the evening. His heart suddenly dropped to the floor.

Pray do not let her have heard a single word which was spoken between myself and Lady Winthrop.

"Lord Bargrave?"

Gentle fingers brushed across his cheek and Giles stepped back suddenly, forcing Lady Winthrop's hand to drop from his arm.

"I... I apologize."

Lady Winthrop's eyes flared wide.

"I do not understand."

"I believe that I cannot do what you ask. Not for this Season, at least. I must... I must remain committed to my niece."

Before he could say anything more, Giles turned around and walked away, leaving Lady Winthrop standing alone. Heat burned in his face, but he did not permit himself to turn back. His mind was scrambling with thoughts, thoughts which he could not quite comprehend. Why he had behaved in such a manner he had very little idea. Why turn away from everything Lady Winthrop had offered him, simply because Miss Lawder had been standing nearby? Why should he care what she thought of him? He was a gentleman in his own right and could do as he wished without fear of censure or disapproval from those lower in rank than he.

And yet, as he walked across the ballroom, Giles became painfully aware that it felt very much as though he were running away. Running away from Miss Lawder, running away from her sharp, astute hazel eyes, and running away from any hint of shame that threatened to capture him.

I have not the smallest consideration for what she thinks, he told himself, marching stiffly across the room. *What she thinks of me has no bearing. I need not give it another thought.*

But as he picked up a glass of champagne, Giles found that his mind was unfortunately clouded by thoughts of none other than Miss Lawder. She refused to remove herself from him, lingering even though she was entirely unwanted - and Giles could not seem to pull his thoughts onto anything else, no matter how hard he tried.

CHAPTER FIVE

*E*mma looked at her reflection in the mirror. A pale face with her hazel eyes as the only color looked back at her.

This is not as enjoyable as I thought it would be.

Heaving a heavy sigh, she picked up the hairbrush and began to run it through her mousy brown hair. It was a little flyaway today, so she pulled it back into a simple chignon. The maid had informed her that Lady Juliet had not yet risen, and thus Emma found herself quite alone. Dressed and prepared for the day, she rose from her chair and walked to the door, intending to make her way to the dining room to break her fast.

But what would happen if Lord Bargrave was already there?

Her hand stilled on the doorknob as an image from the previous evening filled her mind. She had not been looking, had certainly not been studying Lord Bargrave, but had still managed to see him caught in the embrace of another woman. The lady had been fluttering her eyelashes, her hand wrapped around Lord Bargrave's arm while he had leaned his head down and smiled into her eyes. The embarrassment of witnessing such a thing had sent a wave of scorching heat straight through Emma, and she had pulled her gaze away at once - but whether or not Lord Bargrave had seen her fleeting glance, Emma was not yet sure. It had only been when Lady Juliet returned from her dance that Emma had realized Lord Bargrave was no longer standing beside that particular woman. In fact, she had only seen him again on their return to the townhouse, although he had said very little, and had not so much as glanced at her. Coupled with the fact that he had warned her away from accepting another gentleman's attentions - evidently believing that she would be so easily pulled away from her duties - Emma was not at all inclined to be in his company this morning.

Then what if he is already in the breakfast room?

Her stomach grumbled in complaint, and Emma closed her eyes. She could not permit any perceived awkwardness to preventing her from breaking her fast. If Lord Bargrave was already in the breakfast room, then Emma would simply join him and remain as silent as she knew he would wish her to be.

"I have nothing to fear," she told herself sternly. "I have done nothing wrong."

Taking a deep breath, Emma set her shoulders and opened the door. Making her way smartly along the hallway, she pushed open the breakfast room door before she could change her mind and retreat to her bedchamber.

Every fear was answered by Lord Bargrave's presence. His eyes snatched away from the newspaper he had been reading, catching hers for a moment before he cleared his throat and set the newspaper down.

"Good morning."

"Good morning, Lord Bargrave. I come to break my fast. I do hope I am not intruding."

His brows lowered over his eyes, but he waved a hand in her direction.

"Not at all."

He coughed again, and Emma quickly closed the door, aware of the sudden awkwardness between them as it pricked at her skin.

I have never been more aware of a gentleman's dislike than in this moment.

Her resolve to remain silent drained away as she fought to find any way of breaking the tension.

"Lady Juliet did very well last evening." Attempting to keep her voice light, Emma thought to make a few murmurs of conversation, in the hope of ridding them both of the strain which she was convinced he felt also. "I believe that she danced almost every dance."

Lord Bargrave harrumphed, and picked up his newspaper once more, leaving Emma with very little doubt that he was not inclined towards conversation.

I should have remained silent. Quickly filling a plate, she set it on the table and then reached to pour a cup of tea.

"You mistook me yesterday."

Lord Bargrave spoke and set down his newspaper suddenly, looking at her directly. A little surprised, it took Emma a moment to respond.

"I do not know to what you refer."

"At the ball."

Embarrassed, Emma looked away. She had no wish to speak of what she had witnessed between himself and that other lady.

"Your matters are your own, my Lord."

Lord Bargrave cleared his throat gruffly.

"That is not what I am referring to. When I spoke to you about Lord Kincaid, you mistook my meaning entirely."

Something cold ran down the length of Emma's spine.

"You thought I would be pulled from my dedication to your niece by the supposed interest of a gentleman, did you not?"

The feelings which had flooded her the previous evening when Lord Bargrave had first mentioned the gentleman returned to her, and she swallowed hard, her fingers gripping together tightly.

"No, I did not." Lord Bargrave's eyebrows drew together, and his jaw worked for a moment as he held her gaze. "That is why I state that you are mistaken." Emma took a slow breath, seeing the fierceness in his expression and wondering at it. *Is he being truthful? Or is he saying such a thing now so that I do not think ill of him?* "Lord Kincaid is my friend and, therefore, I know him all too well. He is not a gentleman with good motivations when it comes to the young ladies of the *ton*."

Her heart lurched in her chest.

"You mean to say that –"

"Any attention he may offer you comes solely from a desire to facilitate his own pleasures, Miss Lawder."

Fire burned in her chest, sending heat into her face.

"I see."

"I will admit that I was unclear in my conversation with you. I ought to have spoken with clarity but in my concern, I did not."

Emma swallowed hard, no longer able to look into Lord Bargrave's blue-green eyes. Realizing now that he had been doing his best for her in what he had said the previous evening, her embarrassment over what she had said in return came back to her with such force that she found it almost impossible to remain in her seat. Her legs wanted to carry her from the room, wanted to push her away from his company, but yet she remained where she was, her head lowering in mortification.

"Oh!"

"Lord Kincaid is not a gentleman I wish either yourself or Lady Juliet to be in prolonged company with. I hope, in this, you will agree with me."

Emma swallowed against the ache in her throat.

"As I have made quite clear, Lord Bargrave, I will never be distracted or turned from my duties as regards Lady Juliet. You need have no fear of that."

Lord Bargrave picked up his newspaper, opening it again.

"That is good. I doubt such a situation will arise again, but it is a relief to know that you have such a stalwart commitment to my niece."

A shaft of pain dug itself into Emma's heart and, as she stared blankly at her plate, tears began to form in her eyes.

He does not expect such a situation to happen again? I am only worthy of the attention from a rake? He does not think that any other gentleman would ever so much as glance at me?

It was not as though Emma had ever truly considered that this Season could provide something for her - she had never even allowed herself to *think* that she might garner attention from the gentlemen of the *ton*. Her presence here was simply so that she might do all that she could for Lady Juliet – but the fact that Lord Bargrave had said so clearly that he did not expect such a thing to *ever* occur had cut her to the quick. She was only considered, in his eyes, as fodder for gentlemen who were considered both rakes and scoundrels, nothing more. Closing her eyes for a moment,

Emma pushed back her tears with an effort, taking a shaking breath as she did so. When she opened them, Lord Bargrave was still hidden behind his newspaper, setting a wall between them once more. Picking up her teacup, Emma took a small sip and then set it down again – but the ache in her heart did not ease. Whether unwittingly or not, Lord Bargrave had inflicted a very painful wound indeed.

∽

"This is a most *excellent* soiree, is it not?"

Emma forced a smile to her lips.

"I am glad you are enjoying it, Juliet."

The remainder of the day had passed without incident, although Lord Bargrave had not joined them for dinner. A short while thereafter, the ladies had prepared themselves for the evening soiree and Lord Bargrave had been waiting for them in the carriage.

"Lord Blackthorn appears to be a very fine gentleman – and he is unwed, I believe!"

Lady Juliet giggled and grasped Emma's arm, but Emma merely shook her head.

"He is much too old to be suitable for you, my dear. I am not suggesting that he is in his dotage, but certainly, he is a good many years older than you. I do not think that your parents would consent to such a match." Again, Lady Juliet giggled and this time, when Emma looked at her, she saw the teasing smile on her charge's face. "You are teasing me, I see."

"I am." Lady Juliet looped her arm through Emma's. "You have been a little melancholy all day and I am only trying to make you smile. Forgive me if I brought you any concern."

"I shall not be cross with you," Emma replied, as three young ladies began to move towards them. "Forgive me my melancholy, it is not of importance. Come now, there are three young ladies coming to speak to you and you must—"

"Lady Juliet!"

Emma stepped back as her charge immediately moved into the ladies' company, greeting the three ladies in turn. *I am glad she is doing so very well.*

"Good evening, Miss Lawder. I am very glad to see you again."

"Good evening, Lord Wollaston." A little surprised that the gentleman she had been introduced to only yesterday had come to talk with her, Emma gestured towards Lady Juliet. "As you can see, I am with Lady Juliet again this evening."

Having every expectation that the gentleman would wish to go to speak to Lady Juliet almost at once, Emma waited for him to do so, only for the smile on his face to broaden. He was a handsome gentleman, tall and broad-shouldered with dark brown eyes and almost black hair which gleamed in the candlelight.

"I can see that, Miss Lawder. Tell me, are you enjoying the evening? It must be difficult for you to step back into the shadows when you are of a similar age to Lady Juliet."

Emma's breath swirled in her chest.

Pray tell me that he is not a gentleman of a similar ilk to Lord Kincaid.

"I – I am very content, Lord Wollaston."

"That is very good of you to say. Your father is Baron Wakefield, is he not?"

Surprise rushed through her.

"Yes, Lord Wollaston, he is."

"And he has sent you to be a companion rather than come to London for the Season?"

More than a little reluctant to tell Lord Wollaston the truth of her situation, Emma merely shrugged.

"I think that I –"

"It is *most* unfair, is it not?" To Emma's further astonishment, Lady Juliet appeared beside Lord Wollaston, her eyes suddenly bright with interest. "I think that Miss Lawder ought to be here as a lady in her own right, but her father sent her as a companion so that he would not have to bear the expense of the Season."

Emma dropped her head, shame burning a hole in her heart.

Pray do not speak any further, Lady Juliet, she prayed, regretting now that Lady Juliet could be so forthright.

"I see." Lord Wollaston's voice had dropped low and, daring a glance at him, Emma saw how his brows knotted together. Her eyes squeezed closed for a moment. *What must he think of me now?* "Despite your words of contentment, I am certain that you must struggle, Miss Lawder."

Something touched her arm for a brief moment and as Emma opened her eyes, she realized it had been Lord Wollaston. Was his touch meant as an expression of sympathy?

"Miss Lawder is to behave just as I do, however," Lady Juliet continued, in a sing-song voice. "She is to dance and to converse and –"

"That is *not* so, Lady Juliet." Interrupting her charge, Emma tried to speak plainly, recalling her statement to Lord Bargrave earlier that day. "My dear Lady Juliet wishes the best for me but, as it stands, I cannot do as she thinks would be appropriate. My first consideration must be to her. After all, those are my duties, and I should not like to be seen to fail in them."

Lord Wollaston's dark eyes flickered but his smile was soft.

"Your commitment is admirable, Miss Lawder."

"And entirely unnecessary. I have my uncle as my sponsor, of course." Lady Juliet's smile was a little sad, but Emma held her gaze for a long moment, speaking silent words of warning; begging her to say nothing more. "Miss Lawder is quite dedicated to me, as you can see, Lord Wollaston. I believe that her devotion speaks very highly of her character."

"In that, I shall agree with you," came the reply, as Lord Wollaston's easy smile spread across his face. "If you will not dance, Miss Lawder, then I should very much like to often be in conversation with you. Perhaps, after a short while, you will find that Lady Juliet's needs change somewhat, and you will no longer be as... required as you are at present."

Emma did not know what to say, or how to respond. Lord Wollaston appeared to be making it quite plain that he wanted to be often in her company, even though she was a companion – in the hope that, one day, she might be able to be a lady in her own right.

"I do not think that such a thing will ever take place, my Lord." Her voice was a low whisper, her previous embarrassment growing all the stronger. "My father is disinclined towards giving me a place in society. When Lady Juliet weds, then I shall –"

"I shall make certain to keep you as my companion even then, so that you are then free to come to society to seek your own happiness," Lady Juliet declared, interrupting

Emma for the second time. "I think that's only fair, do you not, Lord Wollaston?"

The gentleman's broad smile told Emma that he was firmly in agreement. She, on the other hand, was entirely mortified, wishing that Lady Juliet had chosen not to speak so. She did not want any gentleman to know her particular circumstances - nor any lady for that matter. This was an entirely private matter, and it was not Lady Juliet's place to speak so openly about it.

"Then it seems I shall have to wait for my dance for some time, Miss Lawder." Lord Wollaston shook his head regretfully. "You will find, however, that I am a patient man. If I see something I want, then I will do whatever I can to get it – even if it means waiting for a short while." His smile grew even more as he let his eyes alight on Lady Juliet. "Mayhap Lady Juliet will find a suitable match within the month! And then what will you say, Miss Lawder?"

Emma's smile was unwilling.

"I fear I shall have no other excuse then, Lord Wollaston."

The gentleman did not understand nor recognize her reluctance, for he merely laughed, bowed, and then, to her astonishment, took her hand in his.

"The day that Lady Juliet announces her engagement is the day that you will find me by your side, as I am now," he promised, sending a whirlwind of emotions through Emma. There was no smile on his lips, no, no glint in his eye which spoke of humor. Instead, it seemed to Emma that the gentleman was being entirely serious - and she did not know what to say.

"I shall make haste to find a suitor as soon as possible!" Lady Juliet's laugh broke the tension between Emma and Lord Wollaston, allowing her to drop her head and take a small step back, in the hope that Lady Juliet would continue the conversation without her. "Tell me, Lord Wollaston, should you like –"

"I believe my niece has embarrassed you somewhat."

As Lady Juliet and Lord Wollaston continued to speak, Emma's thoughts were suddenly interrupted by the arrival of Lord Bargrave. Her breath juddered out of her as she looked up into his eyes, seeing them gleam as though he were pleased.

Just how much has he heard?

"Lady Juliet has spoken a little out of turn, that is all."

Lifting her chin a notch, Emma narrowed her eyes as Lord Bargrave chuckled a little darkly.

"And I thought you had no interest in curtailing her somewhat brash manner."

"I do not think that I have said anything of the sort." Folding her arms across her chest, Emma looked at him steadily. "Lady Juliet is doing very well in society, as is evidenced by the amount of interest she has garnered from various gentlemen."

"Including Lord Wollaston?" Lord Bargrave arched one eyebrow. "Or is his attention solely on you?"

Hot tears flooded Emma's eyes, but not from embarrassment, but rather from anger. Lord Bargrave had clearly become aware of Lord Wollaston's interest in her, but appeared now to be suggesting by his tone and expression, that it was somehow her fault.

"I have done nothing to garner any gentleman's interest, Lord Bargrave. I have stated quite clearly to him that there can be no furthering of his interest, such as it is. I have no doubt that you will warn me against him as you have done with Lord Kincaid, but you need not do so. I am as committed to Lady Juliet as I have always been. I have only just finished informing Lord Wollaston that my role as her companion always comes first."

Lord Bargrave's jaw worked, his eyes flashing.

"Ah, but he will wait, will he not?" Throwing out one hand, he gestured towards Lord Wollaston, although his voice was still low. "No doubt you will encourage Lady Juliet into matrimony as soon as you can."

Emma balled both her hands into tight fists.

"How dare you suggest such a thing? How dare you think so little of me? After all that I have said and all that I have done, you still think it right to question my dedication." Aware of the single tear which slipped onto her cheek, Emma wiped it away roughly with the back of her hand. "I am firmly aware of my circumstances. I do not think it probable that I shall ever marry - my father has put an end to that particular dream. But if Lady Juliet is kind enough to grant me the freedom to be in society as myself, then I shall not turn from such an opportunity, should it ever come. Nor will I yearn for such a thing, for I am keenly aware that Lady Juliet's happiness is my only goal. I would never push her towards a gentleman she did not care for, nor whom I believed did not care for her, so that I might find my happiness." Aware that she was speaking at great length, Emma drew in a ragged breath, trying desperately to steady herself whilst keeping her gaze fixed on Lord Bargrave. "Think very carefully, Lord Bargrave. Had I been desperate for Lady Juliet to wed, would I have argued with you about her behaving in this 'brusque manner', as you so call it? Would I not have agreed wholeheartedly and encouraged her fervently to do as you suggested?" Suddenly, Lord Bargrave could no longer look into her eyes. His lips pulled to one side and his eyes turned away from hers as a slow flush began to creep up his neck and into his cheeks. "You have apologized to me once." Taking a few calming breaths, Emma closed her eyes for a moment, pushing back the lingering tears which swelled in her eyes. "And yet you continue to think so little of me. I have no shame of my own. My conscience is clear. I do not think that you can say such a thing yourself."

Assuming that Lord Bargrave would be able to stay near to Lady Juliet, Emma marched past him, threading her way through the other guests. Quite where she was going, she was not entirely sure, but the only thing in her mind was to get as far away from Lord Bargrave as she could. It seemed as though he had learned nothing from their previous discussions and Emma was not sure how she could ever be in his company again.

CHAPTER SIX

"It is quite ridiculous."

Lord Berkshire arched one eyebrow. "To your mind, certainly."

"Whatever does that mean?" Picking up his brandy, Giles threw it back in one gulp. The ball had gone well enough, but he had been desperate to make his way to White's so that he could be away from both his niece and her frustrating companion, particularly after the incident with Lord Wollaston. He had spent the last half an hour telling Lord Berkshire everything, and his friend had listened in near silence. "Do not speak in riddles, I beg you. I am irritable enough already."

Lord Berkshire chuckled, lifting his hand in the direction of a footman so that he might order another brandy.

"Indeed, I can see that you are quite frustrated, and I shall not add to your suffering deliberately." Pausing for a moment, he looked away from Giles, then shrugged one shoulder. "I confess that I must stand on the same side as your niece's companion."

"What?" An explosion of shock sent warmth rushing

through him. "You must be jesting, or you are teasing me, in order to make me all the more frustrated - for your own mirth, no doubt."

Holding up both hands, Lord Berkshire shook his head, even though a grin was spreading across his face.

"I speak no lies, I assure you. First of all, I think you entirely unfair when it comes to the gentleman's interest in Miss Lawder. And secondly, I quite agree that Lady Juliet should be in society as she truly is, rather than play a part for the sake of finding a suitable match. I am aware of your reasons for saying such a thing, but as a married gentleman, I confess that I disagree entirely."

A heavy breath released itself from Giles' lips.

"Had I known you were to disagree with me, I should never have told you of all of this." Slumping back in his chair, he practically snatched the brandy from the footman as he arrived. "I thought I was giving the very best of advice to my niece and now it appears that I have not. It seems that you also believe she ought to behave in this uncouth manner."

Aware that he was being a little dramatic, Giles resisted the urge to roll his eyes at his friend.

"I believe that you had every intention of speaking wisdom," Lord Berkshire told him, his grin fading fast. "But should I have found myself wed to a lady who then turned out to be rather different to the woman I thought her to be... then I believe I would have found myself in a very dark situation indeed."

"But my niece is much too forthright! She speaks her mind, and she acts without consideration for her situation and her standing."

Lord Berkshire's eyes widened slightly.

"Is that so? In what regard?"

Waving a hand, Giles went into a long and convoluted explanation about what had occurred during the first day of Lady Juliet's arrival.

"She had the companion's things moved into another bedchamber without even consulting me," He finished expecting Lord Berkshire to shake his head and frown at Lady Juliet's behavior. "It was utterly ridiculous."

His friend considered for a short while but did not give the immediate response that Giles had expected.

"I must confess that I am a little surprised to hear that you treated the companion in such a way. I cannot imagine why you would not give her a proper room."

"Because she is a *paid* companion! As far as I am concerned, she does not need the very best, but also will not be given the very worst. I assumed the bedchamber which I had offered her was more than suitable."

"Tell me, does she come from a titled family?"

Shrugging, Giles swirled the brandy in his glass.

"She is only the daughter of a Baron." Guilt pricked his conscience over his dismissive attitude towards the lady, but he told himself that he had no reason to feel such a thing. "I will admit that I am surprised at how youthful she is. I had expected her to be older than myself, but it seems that she is only a few years older than Lady Juliet. However, none of that is of any importance – she is still a paid companion and I feel quite justified in my decision."

"And this is also why you insist that she must behave in such a reclusive manner around any gentleman who shows her even the smallest interest?"

Giles shrugged and ignored the continuing prickling of guilt in his heart.

"Her duty is to my niece."

"But yet you yourself have said that she has shown no

delight in any gentleman. Any interest given to her, she has rebuffed gently. By her words and by her actions she has made it plain that she is dedicated to your niece."

"Yes, that is so. But a lady can be easily persuaded, can she not?"

The heavy burden on his shoulders seemed to drop all the more weightily down upon him.

A small smile flickered across his friend's face.

"It seems as though you feel quite justified. Do you still wish for my opinion?"

"Only so that I may inform my niece that she is mistaken in her behavior."

Lord Berkshire chuckled.

"You and I have been friends for some time, and I know that you are not as haughty as you sound. However, out of concern for such arrogant sounding words, I have no hesitation in informing you that I think you are quite wrong. This paid companion is just as much a lady as your niece."

Giles' shoulders slumped.

"I see."

"The young lady is the daughter of a Baron, and I assume that circumstances have forced her into such a position."

One eyebrow arched and Giles had no other option but to nod.

"From what I understand, her father considered her a burden. Hence why I considered that she would be a good deal older, why I believed she would be a spinster."

He spoke lightly, but his heart twisted as he thought of what she must have endured. *Why did I never consider her position in such a light before?*

A flicker of compassion grew in Lord Berkshire's eyes.

"That must be very difficult indeed for the young lady. I

confess that I am surprised by you. You ought to be treating her with sympathy and compassion, and as much understanding as possible. Why then do you treat her with such disregard?"

The gentle rebuke burned like fire in Giles's heart. His anger and his frustration died away as he looked into Lord Berkshire's face and saw there the sympathy for Miss Lawder, which he ought to be feeling himself.

"Because..." Groaning, he passed one hand over his eyes, loath to admit the truth. "Because I have no wish to be sponsoring my niece into society. I am frustrated at her presence here. I am irritated at how much I must give up. I had been greatly anticipating the London Season for many reasons and now I find that what I had hoped for cannot be... simply because I have my niece and her companion residing with me."

Something stabbed at him hard, and he winced.

And for whatever reason, I do not like the fact that other gentlemen of the ton *notice her.*

Lord Berkshire spread his hands, one eyebrow lifting.

"I am afraid I have very little sympathy for you, my friend. This is a situation of your own making. You wrote to your sister and said that you would take on your niece. Why now are you complaining? And what is worse - why are you treating the companion as though *she* is the cause of all of your frustrations?"

For what was the second time, Giles's heart burned with guilt. Taking a sip of his Brandy, he let his friend's words seep down into his soul, realizing that he had been very foolish indeed.

"I think that this companion has a good deal more wisdom than you credit her with. I believe that she is quite right to tell you that you ought *not* to encourage your niece to pretend she is a mild, quiet sort when she is precisely the opposite. That will not make for a happy marriage, And regardless of your own selfishness, surely you can see that being herself would be the very best for Lady Juliet."

"I believe that you have rebuked me enough, old friend." Throwing back the rest of his Brandy, Giles set down the empty glass on the table beside him. "I have been shown the error of my ways."

Lord Berkshire grinned.

"Then mayhap you realize that the only reason you are encouraging your niece to behave in such a way is so that she might make a match all the more quickly. And thus you will be free of her all the sooner. It is not Miss Lawder who wishes for her freedom. It is you." Scowling, Giles shook his head to himself, but did not refute the idea. "Forgive me, I ought not to go on."

"I appreciate your candor, even though it may not appear so." Forcing a smile, Giles rose from his chair. "It seems I have much to think on and I cannot do so here. Might I see you tomorrow, at Lord Johnston's ball?"

His friend nodded.

"My wife and I will be in attendance. Perhaps you may do us the honor of introducing us to your niece and her companion."

"I should be glad to introduce you to Lady Juliet."

"And also to her companion?"

Lord Berkshire waited as Giles closed his eyes, letting out a breath of frustration through clenched teeth. Again, it seemed that he had made a mistake.

"Yes, I shall introduce Miss Lawder tomorrow also. Thank you and good evening."

With a broad smile, Lord Berkshire lifted a hand in Giles' direction.

"Good evening. I look forward to seeing you again come the morrow."

Letting out a long sigh, Giles made his way from White's and back towards his carriage. He had gone in search of his friend in the hope that he would listen to his frustrations and agree with everything he said. However, quite the opposite had taken place, and he was now returning home with a very heavy heart indeed.

"I shall have to apologize to her."

Muttering to himself, Giles ran one hand over his face as he sat back in his carriage, leaning against the squabs. The thought of having to admit to a mere companion that she had been correct in her judgments, whilst he had been entirely mistaken, was a great weight on his conscience. The truth was that he had no desire to speak to her so, yet he knew that it was the honorable thing for him to do. He had made a mistake - had made more than one mistake, in fact, and Miss Lawder deserved an apology.

I shall not be tardy in giving it, no matter my reluctance.

Taking in a deep breath, Giles closed his eyes, one hand curling into a fist as his determination grew.

I can only hope that Miss Lawder will be willing to listen and to forgive.

∽

"Good evening, My Lord."

"I am a little surprised to see you." Shrugging out of his coat, Giles handed it to his butler. "I did inform you that I would be late to return and that the staff need not stay awake on my account, did I not?"

"You did, my Lord."

No other explanation was given as to the butler's presence and Giles hid a smile, all too aware of the butler's loyalty.

"I shall rise late, come the morrow. I am certain that my niece and Miss Lawder will do the same and therefore the staff need not rise too early."

The butler nodded, a flicker of a smile on his lips for a brief moment.

"Thank you, my Lord."

"I shall take a brandy in the library before I retire."

"Yes, my Lord. I should also inform you that Miss Lawder is presently in the library, however."

Surprise jerked through Giles' frame.

"Miss Lawder is not yet abed?"

"No, my Lord. I believe she was having trouble sleeping, so I suggested a little warm milk and a book might be of aid to her. She is presently perusing the books in the library, whilst the milk is being prepared. If you wish, I can inform her of your presence."

Knowing that Miss Lawder would immediately scuttle back to her bedchamber should the butler do so, Giles shook his head. It appeared that an excellent opportunity for his apology had presented itself, and he was not about to avoid it.

"I shall speak with her before she retires. You need not linger. Once the milk has been prepared, there will be no other duties required of you."

The butler nodded.

"Thank you, my Lord. I shall fetch it at once."

The thought of speaking to Miss Lawder in such a contrite fashion had Giles recoiling somewhat, but he forced his steps in the direction of the library, regardless. Remembering how Lord Berkshire had warned him of his arrogance, Giles drew in a deep breath as he knocked lightly on the library door before stepping inside.

A figure clad in white whirled towards him, her eyes wide. Miss Lawder's light brown hair was braided down around one shoulder, and she was swathed in her nightrail and wrap. Her hazel eyes were wide with astonishment, and her cheeks suddenly burned a furious red.

Giles cleared his throat. For whatever reason, he had not even considered that the lady would be in her night things, nor given the smallest thought to how awkward a situation this might now be. He had only considered his need to apologize - but now that he stood in the library with her, Giles realized just how inappropriate a situation this was.

"Miss Lawder." Clasping his hands behind his back, he turned his head so that he would not be looking directly at her. "The butler informed me that you were here."

"I..." Miss Lawder's voice was a broken whisper. "I could not sleep, so I thought that I... forgive me, I ought not to be here. I should have asked for your permission before I –"

"Pray do not upset yourself." Making certain to keep his eyes trained on the fireplace, Giles swiped one hand through the air between them. "I am not at all upset. You are welcome to use the library as often as you wish. I thought to come and spend a little time with you before I retired."

He heard a swift intake of breath coming from the lady just as a frown drew itself across his brow.

"It seemed to me like a good opportunity since you are unable to sleep and I only just returned from White's," he began, concerned now that his previous behavior would render her disinclined to listen to him now. "I hope that you are willing, Miss Lawder?"

Miss Lawder's breathing was quickening now, to the point that Giles could not help but turn his gaze towards her. Rather than having a flush of red in her cheeks, her face was stark white, and her hands clasped tightly below her chin.

"I understand that you think ill of me. That is to be expected and I do not shy away from such a perspective. I only ask that you give me an opportunity to prove just how considerate I may be - particularly now that I have had the opportunity to consider my previous behavior. I am certain that our relationship may be a good deal warmer, should you grant me the opportunity."

Much to Giles's frustration, Miss Lawder's eyes widened to such an extent that her entire expression was one of sheer horror.

It appears that no matter what I say, she will think poorly of me. Attempting to order his thoughts so that he might come up with further explanation, Giles' attention was caught when Miss Lawder took three hurried steps backwards, stumbling as she did so. On instinct he stepped forward, but Miss Lawder let out a soft cry of fear, her hands clenching under her chin once more as she backed away, her eyes still huge.

"Whatever is the matter?" A trifle irritated, Giles stopped still, his arms folded tightly across his chest as he glared at the young woman in front of him. "Here I am trying to apologize and –"

"I am not that sort of companion, my Lord. I am not that sort of lady!"

Miss Lawder's wide eyes met his and for the first time, Giles saw her tremble. All irritation left him at once, washed away by the sudden and stark realization of what she now thought of him.

"I beg of you to please let me return to my bedchamber."

Giles closed his eyes, shoving both hands through his hair as a growl of frustration left his lips. This, however, elicited another cry from Miss Lawder and upon opening his eyes, Giles saw her begin to try to edge past him, making for the door.

"Wait a moment!"

His loud exclamation had her stop dead, though her eyes were still fixed on the door. Realizing now that he stood directly in her path to the door and freedom, Giles stepped to one side and spread both his hands wide.

"Forgive me." Dropping his hands, he shook his head. "I do not mean to prevent you from leaving, Miss Lawder. Nor do I mean to suggest or… ask that you offer me anything of yourself. That is a mistake on my part. I have not explained myself clearly enough."

Taking another step backward so that she would see he was genuine, Giles waited for a few moments for Miss Lawder to react. Her eyes remained huge, but she dropped her hands from her chin and clasped them tightly in front of her instead.

"I came here only to apologize, Miss Lawder. That is the truth of it. My words have been muddled and, therefore, your perception of me is confused. I do not come here with any other intention than to tell you that I am sorry for my previous behavior and to hope that you might be willing to forgive me so that our association can be more amicable." Licking his lips, he shrugged both shoulders and then took one final step backward. "It seems that even with such good intentions, I have managed to twist things terribly. I must apologize for this also."

Silence fell, although Giles could still hear Miss Lawder's quick breaths. He did not know where to look, mortification beginning to squeeze at his heart, sending a billowing cloud of heat up into his face. He had been thoughtless, careless, and inconsiderate to the point of frightening Miss Lawder terribly. He would not blame her if she ran from the library, and did not wish to ever see him alone again.

"You... you wish to apologize?"

Her voice was a little louder now and when Giles looked towards her, he was relieved to see the small spot of color coming back into her cheeks.

"Yes." Taking in a deep breath, he spread his hands. *I must be entirely honest.* "Yes, Miss Lawder. I wish to apologize, for I have been inconsiderate and selfish. I will admit to you that I found myself irritated at the prospect of having my niece here - even though I agreed to such a thing myself! I have always looked forward to the London Season for it is a time when I am free of responsibilities. Now, however, I find myself with the responsibility of a niece, whom I must do all I can for, if she is to marry well."

"But... but you knew that she was to attend London for the Season. You knew that there would be some things you would have to give up."

Giles sighed and closed his eyes.

"Yes, it is as you say. In speaking with my friend, Lord Berkshire, I was made to see just how selfish and ridiculous my behavior has been. In addition, I have not shown you the respect that your position deserves." He dropped his hands to his side. "It appears that you have been quite right in your advice with regard to Lady Juliet and her character. Lady Juliet was right to move your bedchamber to one much more suitable. And I, in all things, appear to have been quite mistaken. Even though it seems I cannot even apologize without blundering!" Miss Lawder's eyes remained rather large, but there was no fear in her expression any longer. A gentle calm filled the room and Giles' chest expanded as he drew in along steadying breath. At least he had been able to say everything he had wanted, even if it had caused a great misunderstanding initially. "I do not have anything else to say and nor would I keep you here without reason. I shall bid you goodnight."

Miss Lawder hurried forward, going to the door before he could reach it.

"I will take my leave and retire to bed, my Lord. Pray, do not let me keep you from your library."

Giles hesitated, then nodded.

"Very well. Thank you. Miss Lawder."

Her hand on the doorknob, she turned to face him. Her gaze was steady as she looked at his face, her lower lip caught between her teeth. Waiting expectantly, Giles clasped both hands behind his back, wondering what it was that she wished to say. A minute or so of silence passed and still, Miss Lawder said nothing. Then straightening her shoulders, she inclined her head for a moment.

"I am very grateful to you. Your apology appears sincere, and I am gratified."

"It is entirely sincere, I assure you."

Miss Lawder took in another breath and a hint of a smile danced across her lips.

"Then let us hope we might be civil for the next few weeks, for Lady Juliet's sake."

"Perhaps we might aim for something a little more than merely civil." The words were out of his mouth before Giles could prevent them, before he had even had opportunity to think of what he was saying. "That is, I mean... if you should wish for such a thing." Miss Lawder's smile faded but her gaze remained fixed on his. Was that a glimmer of interest in her eyes? "I mean to say that perhaps we might consider being friends."

The moment the words fell from his mouth, Giles winced visibly. They sounded so trite, almost child-like in their request.

But much to his astonishment, the smile quickly returned to Miss Lawder's face. It seemed that she did not think him trite at all.

"I think that is something I should like. It would be far better than mere civility, I suppose."

"I think it would be, yes."

Miss Lawder's smile grew until her hazel eyes were bright and vivid.

"Then I accept that offer, Lord Bargrave. I do hope that we can begin to build on such a foundation from the morrow."

Giles bowed, relief flooding his soul. It felt as though he were stepping out into a brand-new morning, taking a breath of the fresh, clean summer air.

"Thank you. You have a generous heart, Miss Lawder. I am grateful that my sister has employed you as companion. I believe that Lady Juliet is in the very best of company."

When he glanced up at her again, a flush had danced across her cheeks but in the next moment she was gone from the room, closing the door tightly behind her. Giles made his way to a chair and slumped down in it - but rather than a frown on his face, there remained a small smile of relief. From tomorrow, everything would begin anew, and for that, he was beyond grateful.

CHAPTER SEVEN

How strange it is that a gentleman can appear so very different after only a single conversation.

Emma permitted her gaze to linger on Lord Bargrave as his eyes flicked between Lady Juliet and Lord Harrogate – the gentleman who had come to call only a few minutes earlier. For the first time since she had arrived in London, her heart was at peace. There was no underlying tension, there were no whispers of strain and stress which seemed to tug at every sinew. Instead, it felt as though she could breathe a little easier now, as if she were finally able to relax in Lord Bargrave's home. And all because he had sought her out to give her a very simple apology.

Her lips lifted at the edges.

Once I had overcome my fear and realized that he was not attempting to seduce me, I thought he spoke very well.

Even now, she could see the shock which had come into his expression as she had stepped back, afraid of what he might do. It had been in that moment she had realized that her fears were entirely unfounded - he had not been attempting to do anything of the sort. Rather, in a most convoluted manner, he had been trying to apologize - and how grateful she was for it.

"Lord Harrogate appears a most... devoted gentleman."

Speaking out of the corner of his mouth, Lord Bargrave shot her a quick glance. Emma did not know what to say at first, then caught the glint in his eye and found herself smiling.

"Indeed," she answered softly so that Lord Harrogate would not overhear. "He appears to be most intrigued with every single word which is uttered from Lady Juliet's mouth!"

At this Lord Bargrave grinned, his eyes dancing with mirth. Thus far, Lord Harrogate had uttered only a brief word of greeting to both Emma and Lord Bargrave, and since then, had spent every single moment in conversation with Lady Juliet. In fact, Emma was quite convinced that the gentleman had not even lifted his gaze from Lady Juliet for a single second. Either he was incredibly devoted to her, or he was rather desperate for her attention... Emma simply could not decide which.

"Mayhap I ought to remind him that other gentlemen are coming to call very soon." Lord Bargrave's smile continued to linger, although his eyes remained steadily fixed on his niece. "Or that he has not taken a single sip of his tea."

Emma lifted her hand to her mouth, hiding her smile.

"I am convinced that neither thing will move him from Lady Juliet's company."

Their eyes met for a brief second and Emma was startled by the warmth that she saw in Lord Bargrave's gaze. In fact, his broad smile seemed to change his entire expression. Any coldness that she had once seen in his blue eyes was now quite gone, replaced instead by a brilliant light which seemed to shine out towards her. A dimple caught one cheek as he smiled, and Emma found herself a little surprised by just how handsome he now appeared. It truly was astonishing just how much had changed between them.

"Alas, I fear you must now take your leave."

Emma's eyes flew to Lady Juliet. To her astonishment, her charge had already risen from her chair, and Lord Harrogate was stammering something as he too rose from his seat.

"I am expecting another gentleman caller, you understand." Lady Juliet dipped into a curtsey before Emma had even risen to her feet. "It was very pleasant to talk with you this afternoon, Lord Harrogate. Thank you for calling."

Lord Bargrave, who had also risen, dropped into a bow.

"Yes, thank you for calling, Lord Harrogate. You are welcome to call again any time you wish."

Seeing the way that Lady Juliet's eyes flared in evident horror, Emma bobbed a curtsey so that the gentleman would not see her smile.

"Good afternoon, Lord Harrogate."

The gentleman took a step backward, mumbled something under his breath, and then bowed toward Lord Bargrave. He appeared entirely discomposed, most likely due to the way that Lady Juliet had ended their conversation so abruptly.

"Good afternoon to you all."

His words were short and clipped, and he strode from the room in quick steps, his back very straight indeed. The moment that the door closed, Emma threw up her hands as Lady Juliet flopped back into her chair with a heavy sigh.

"I take it, then, that you have a very little time for Lord Harrogate's company?"

Lady Juliet rolled her eyes as Lord Bargrave took his seat again.

"I found him very severe in his interest and conversation. I do not believe that he said even a single word to you!"

"That is because I am your companion. Why should he speak to me when you are present?"

Lord Bargrave cleared his throat.

"Forgive me, but I would disagree with you on that point. Any man who claims to be a gentleman ought to speak to the lady who holds his interest *as well as* her companion - or whoever else is present."

A little uncertain as to whether or not he was saying such a thing to garner her good favor, Emma could not help but smile at him, aware of a strange quickening in her chest.

"That is very kind of you to say, but it is clear that Lord Harrogate only did so simply because he was quite taken with Lady Juliet."

"But I am not at all taken with him." Smiling, Lady Juliet placed both hands delicately in her lap, then shrugged one shoulder. "There was no need to further the conversation. I hope that he will understand my feelings and will not call again *despite* my uncle's insistence that he is free to do so whenever he wishes."

This was followed by a sharp look in Lord Bargrave's direction but much to Emma's surprise, Lord Bargrave only laughed. It was a rich, full sound which seemed to fill the room and caused her to tip up the corners of her mouth in response.

"I believe that you have made things quite clear, my dear girl - I must confess that I cannot fault you."

Lady Juliet's eyes rounded suddenly, and her smile faded.

"Good gracious." Blinking, she shook her head. "That is

very generous of you to say, Uncle. I confess that I am a little surprised to hear such a thing."

A gentle flush warmed Emma's cheeks as Lord Bargrave looked towards her.

"I have been convinced that I was in the wrong to ever suggest that you be quiet and biddable in the first place," he told his niece whilst still regarding Emma carefully. "I can only beg your forgiveness, as I have done with Miss Lawder."

Emma felt rather than saw Lady Juliet's eyes lingering upon her, searching her face and expression. Forcing a smile, she waited for Lady Juliet to respond, seeing how the girl tipped her head slightly to one side as though she might be able to understand the situation a little better.

"You have already spoken to Miss Lawder, Uncle?"

Lord Bargrave nodded.

"I have."

"And I have accepted his apology," Emma put in, wanting the conversation to come to a swift end before her charge could ask her about *when* such a discussion had taken place.

"I see." A bright smile spread across Lady Juliet's face. "Then that will explain the sunny ambience which has spread across this house since this morning."

A little surprised, Emma shared a look with Lord Bargrave, then turned her eyes away, her flushed cheeks growing all the hotter.

"I am glad that you feel it so," She heard Lord Bargrave say, while she dropped her gaze to her lap. "I apologize, Lady Juliet, for my attitude, and my lack of consideration, which has been so apparent since the very first moment of your arrival. I can assure you that such behaviors will no longer be evident. I have seen the error of my ways and must apologize profusely."

Lady Juliet rose, walked across the room, and pressed a kiss to her uncle's cheek.

"Of course, uncle. I am only glad that the situation has been resolved so amicably--- and I am all too aware that my frankness can, at times, be somewhat difficult. I am willing to take guidance from you, Uncle, so long as you do not push such a trait away from me entirely."

Lord Bargrave's smile was an easy one.

"I am certain that things between us will be more felicitous from now on, my dear niece. There shall be harmony in this household from this day forward!"

Emma beamed in delight as Lady Juliet returned to her seat. It felt as though everything had begun all over again, as though this was the first time that she had been introduced to Lord Bargrave. There was a kindness to his character which she had not seen before, for it had been hidden by his frustration, and Emma found herself looking forward to getting to know the gentleman a little more over her time in London.

A tap came at the door.

"Yes?"

The butler entered the room.

"There is a visitor, my Lord."

"Send them in." Lord Bargrave sighed and shifted in his chair. "Shall every afternoon be as this, do you think, Miss Lawder? Shall I have to sit here every day and watch as gentleman after gentleman comes to call upon my niece?"

Emma laughed softly as Lady Juliet rolled her eyes, although her smile was quick to flit across her lips.

"My Lord, it is not a —"

"Hurry, do not be tardy." Interrupting the butler, Lord

Bargrave chuckled as the man turned on his heel and made his way back to the door. "The sooner we have the next gentleman caller, the better."

As the door opened again, Emma rose to her feet alongside Lord Bargrave and Lady Juliet, expecting there to be another gentleman to greet. Lord Bargrave had not taken the gentleman's card from the butler So as yet, none of them knew who this gentleman might be.

Except it was not a gentleman.

"Lady... Fullerton."

Lord Bargrave's voice was suddenly strangled, and it took him a moment to bow towards the lady.

"Forgive me. I have not been introduced to your... present company."

Emma glanced toward Lord Bargrave and saw the flush of red in his face as he quickly made the introductions. She dropped into a curtsey as was required and then took her seat, murmuring only a quiet greeting. Whoever this lady was, she perhaps had not expected Lord Bargrave to be in company, for the smile on her lips did not bring any light to her eyes. She was a willowy figure with astonishingly bright blue eyes, a head covered in golden curls and, from the cut of her clothes, Emma assumed that she was the lady of the highest quality.

"I did not know that you had returned to London." Lord Bargrave reached to ring the bell for tea and then dropped back into his seat. "Are you here for the Season?"

"I am. I have my daughter with me also."

Emma blinked rapidly, glancing at Lady Juliet, and seeing the same surprise etched in her features. Lady Fullerton did not appear old enough to have a daughter ready for the London Season. In fact, the lady was surely only a few years older than Lady Juliet herself!

"I see. And has your daughter come out as yet?"

Lady Fullerton shook her head, her smile a little tight.

"That is why I have come to call, Lord Bargrave. An invitation to a ball was sent to you some weeks ago, but as yet you have not responded. I know that my husband would be greatly delighted should you be able to attend - and the invitation of course extends to your niece also."

Something heavy dropped into Emma's stomach, for it seemed quite plain that Lady Fullerton did not wish Emma to be in attendance. That might well be simply because the number of guests attending was already significant, and to add two further guests would be a little much – but from the sidelong glance that Lady Fullerton shot her, Emma was not fully convinced that this was the sole cause.

"I am terribly sorry. I do not recall such an invitation, but I am quite certain that we can *all* attend."

The emphasis in Lord Bargrave's voice sent Emma's heart into a sudden flutter. She raised her eyes to his for a moment and saw him look towards her also. There was steel in his gaze, which she had not expected. It was as though he was suddenly determined to make certain that she was always fully included, as he now believed she ought to be - and Emma found herself all the more grateful to him.

"That is very kind of you." A touch of coolness came into Lady Fullerton's voice, but her lips remained curved into a smile. "I am sorry if the invitation has gone missing, although that would explain your lack of response. I am very glad to hear that you will be able to attend after all. My daughter will, of course, be just as delighted."

Lord Bargrave smiled but did not say anything further. Emma shivered, her skin prickling as a shadow seemed to fall across the room, blocking the sunlight from the windows. Even Lady Juliet remained silent, having not said a single word since Lady Fullerton's arrival. Catching her charge's eye, Emma saw the questions written there but found that she could not answer any of them. There was something between Lady Fullerton and Lord Bargrave, something which remained - as yet - quite unsaid. For a moment, a vision of Lord Bargrave and the lady he had been speaking to the previous evening fell back into her mind and Emma dropped her gaze to her hands, her teeth catching her bottom lip. She had seen the interest in Lord Bargrave's eyes when he had been speaking to that particular lady - was it possible that Lady Fullerton had seen it also? Had she been present? And had she previously been close to Lord Bargrave, and was now jealous of the interest he had shown to another?

"I shall take up no more of your time." Rising to her feet, Lady Fullerton dropped into a curtsey, but her smile was entirely absent. "I shall send you another invitation the moment I return home. Thank you, Lord Bargrave, Lady Juliet."

To Emma, she said, not a word.

Turning swiftly, Lady Fullerton made her way to the door and left the room without a second glance, leaving Emma and Lady Juliet to stare after her.

"Good gracious, she is a most extraordinary woman!" Lady Juliet, with her usual frankness, spread her hands wide as she turned back to her uncle. "I think that she was a little displeased with you."

Lord Bargrave shrugged and shook his head.

"It is hardly my fault if her invitation has gone missing. Although I think it very fair that we attend, I do hope you shall not mind."

"I shall not mind in the least!" Lady Juliet exclaimed, sitting back down in her chair.

"Might I ask what her daughter's name is?"

Clasping her hands tightly together, Emma waited for Lord Bargrave to answer her question. He did not do so immediately, but instead rose from his chair and walked across the room to pick up a brandy glass.

"She is Lady Sarah Ann, daughter to the Earl of Fullerton. She is his daughter from a previous marriage, whereas Lady Fullerton is her stepmother. I believe his first wife died shortly after the child was born."

"I see." Emma licked her lips, wondering why Lord Bargrave had not looked at her for a single moment since Lady Fullerton's arrival. "That is a great shame."

"Although it does explain my astonishment when I looked at the lady and thought her incapable of having a daughter so close to her own age!"

Lady Juliet laughed, and Emma looked away, grimacing just a little. Whilst it did answer that question. It did not answer what there had been between Lady Fullerton and Lord Bargrave. There had been something, certainly, for the room would not have filled with such tension, had there been only an acquaintance.

It is not my place to know nor to question.

Taking a deep breath, Emma squared her shoulders.

"I am sure that there will be another gentleman caller very soon. Lady Juliet. Did not Lord Bridgewater say that he would call also?"

Lady Juliet smiled, the subject of Lady Fullerton quite forgotten.

"He did, as did Lord Netherton."

"Then I suggest that you take a short turn about the room whilst you wait."

Lady Juliet smiled and nodded before rising to her feet and wandering across the room towards her uncle. Emma kept her gaze far from Lord Bargrave, silencing the questions which built continually in her mind. His connection with Lady Fullerton had no bearing on her presence in London, nor on her role as regarded Lady Juliet. Whatever was troubling him about the lady had nothing whatsoever to do with Emma, and she reminded herself that to show even the smallest flicker of interest might cause her trouble. They had only just found themselves at a happy equilibrium, and Emma was determined that she would not risk setting them all off-balance again.

CHAPTER EIGHT

Taking a sip of his wine, Giles let his eyes follow Miss Lawder as she crossed the room. The afternoon soiree at Lord Nelson's house had been a welcome distraction from his tumultuous thoughts. Ever since Lady Fullerton had arrived at his door, Giles had found himself struggling to understand her sudden eagerness for his presence.

And to invite me to a ball for her stepdaughter? The thought sent his brows tumbling close together as he scowled to himself. *That is very strange indeed.*

His thoughts of Lady Fullerton were suddenly interrupted as he saw Miss Lawder laugh, her head lifting slightly as her eyes sparkled. Her lips pulled wide and the freedom in her expression sent a small smile to his lips.

"Whatever it is that you are looking at, it must bring you great delight, for I do not think I have seen you smile in such a way for a long time."

Hastily rearranging his features, Giles turned sharply away from Miss Lawder.

"I was not watching anyone. I was merely thinking of..."

To his horror, his mind suddenly went blank, and Lord Berkshire chuckled, putting one hand on Giles' shoulder.

"Whilst you come up with some excuse. I shall tell you that I think that you were looking directly towards your niece's companion." His grin spread as Giles shook his head fervently. "Although I see that you are determined not to admit it."

Hitting upon an idea, Giles shrugged his shoulders.

"You may be convinced of it, but you are quite mistaken. In truth, I was thinking of Lady Fullerton."

In an instant, the smile fled from Lord Berkshire's face.

"Lady Fullerton? Whyever should you be thinking of her?"

"Because she came to call upon me yesterday." Seeing his friend's eyebrows lift, Giles let out a small sigh. "I was as astonished as you. It has been some years since I was last in her company, and as you know, we did not part amicably."

Lord Berkshire nodded.

"She threw herself at you and you refused to accept her attentions. At the time, you were convinced that she sought to find a way to become your bride."

Giles nodded, his lips thinning as he recalled the lady. It had been some five years ago. Lady Fullerton – or Miss Jennings, as she had been then - had certainly caught his eye. She had been described as a diamond of the first water, and Giles had been interested in making her acquaintance, but given that he never concerned himself with young women making their come out, he had never pursued her further. Yes, there had been some dances and a few simple flirtations, but that had been all he had offered her. He could still recall the night of his soiree when she had found him walking in the garden and had thrust herself into his arms, in an apparent moment of weakness. It had been dark and, for the first few moments, Giles had found himself reacting to the soft arms around his neck and the whispered words of affection. But then he had realized who it was, and had hastily stepped back from her, filled with both fear and horror. Fear that he would be caught, that he would be trapped, that he would be forced into matrimony with a lady he barely knew and certainly did not care for. She had cried out for him, but Giles had stumbled back inside with all speed, making his presence known among his guests so that they all knew he was moving amongst them rather than with her.

"It has been some years since she has been in London, has it not?"

"I believe so. She is wed to Lord Fullerton now and has a stepdaughter to care for."

Lord Berkshire grimaced.

"I recall that Lord Fullerton is many years older than his wife. How did such a match come about?"

"I presume that her father arranged it. After that night, I took very little interest in the lady and made it my purpose never to be in company with her. Which is why I find it very strange indeed that she should appear at my door with the request that I attend her stepdaughter's ball."

Nodding, his friend looked away, rubbing his chin with one hand.

"That is most peculiar." His eyes did not fix to any one thing but darted around the room. "Did you accept?"

"I had no other choice but to do so. My niece and her companion were present in the room at the time, and I could not refuse without garnering many questions from my niece. Besides," he shrugged, "Mayhap she wishes to extend some good grace towards me. Perhaps she seeks to forget the past and this is her way of doing so."

Lord Berkshire murmured his agreement, but did not appear convinced. Instead, his eyes remained searching, his brow furrowing.

"I should still be on your guard. You know very little about the lady, save for the fact that she was manipulative enough to try to trap you into marriage. What is there to say that she is not doing the same now?"

Giles grinned and shook his head, finding a little humor in the situation.

"Perhaps because she is already married?" His eyebrow lifted, his grin spreading wider. "I hardly think that she will be trying to trap me into matrimony again."

"You may laugh, but there is wisdom in what I suggest. There are other ways to trap a gentleman. You must be on your guard."

The smile on Giles' lips began to fade and he dropped his gaze from his friend's dark expression.

"I shall be. You need not have any doubt about that."

"Good." Lord Berkshire suddenly slapped Giles on the shoulder, making him jump. "Now that we have discussed this serious matter, you may inform me of why you find Miss Lawder so very fascinating."

Giles looked away sharply, running one hand over his mouth.

"I have no interest in Miss Lawder. I have apologized to her and that has done very well for us both. These last two days have been quite... contented."

Hearing his friend chuckle, Giles kept his eyes trained on someone in the corner of the room rather than look into his friend's eyes.

"Contented?"

"It is better than having many arguments. I will admit to

you, however, that your advice has been invaluable. I thank you for that."

Glancing toward Lord Berkshire, Giles did his best to ignore the broad grin which was spreading across his friend's face.

He may think what he wishes. I have no interest in Miss Lawder.

But even as he thought those words, Giles found his heart twisting painfully. Shaking his head to himself, he clenched his hands into tight fists. It could not be. He could not find himself at all interested in his niece's companion, particularly after what he had said to her previously. That would be disastrous indeed.

∽

"Good evening, Lord Bargrave."

Giles started violently, surprising Lady Winthrop, who took a small step backward in response.

"Good evening, Lady Winthrop." Covering his reaction with a swift bow, Giles pushed away his embarrassment. "Are you enjoying the soiree?"

"I should enjoy it a good deal more, if I had better company."

The glint in Lady Winthrop's eyes left Giles in no doubt as to what she was referring to. In a previous Season, he had often escaped with her to a quiet spot so that he might indulge in a few kisses. Now, however, he found such an idea almost repugnant. There was no curl of delight in his belly, no flare of excitement that spread through his veins. Instead, he found his heart a little heavy, pushing downwards in his chest.

Was I really that sort of gentleman? The kind who

would only take his own pleasures without thought or genuine consideration?

Reminded of Lord Berkshire's gentle questions as to whether selfishness and arrogance were becoming a part of his character, Giles drew in a deep breath.

"Lady Winthrop, I –"

"I know that you were about to accept my offer of company the last time we spoke but we were interrupted by your niece and her companion. Given that I can see them both in deep conversation with another lady, I hardly think they will miss you, should you step away for a few moments."

Her hand strayed to his arm, her fingers pressing lightly against his wrist before moving to brush his own fingers. Giles did not move, and certainly did not return the gesture, suddenly seeing his past behavior in an entirely new – and somewhat disturbing – light.

"Again, I must decline." Seeing her lips bunch together in a pout, Giles shook his head. He had to make his position quite clear so that this would not happen again. "Lady Winthrop, I cannot be to you what I was in the past. You will find that I am something of a reformed gentleman, in fact." This was a very swift change of character, but Giles was suddenly determined to behave with all propriety. "I must care for my niece. My only purpose in London at present is to make certain that she does well in society."

Lady Winthrop arched one eyebrow.

"But should she make her match....?"

"I cannot say whether that will occur this Season or the next, or mayhap the Season after. Regardless, I am quite devoted to my niece and to her happiness. I shall guide her towards the very best of gentlemen, and therefore Lady Winthrop, I too, must become the very best of gentlemen."

He searched her eyes and saw the surprise glisten there. Her hand left his and she took a small step back.

"You quite astonished me. Lord Bargrave. I must admit that I am a little disappointed."

"I am afraid I cannot prevent that." A sudden movement caught his attention and he looked over Lady Winthrop's shoulder to see Miss Lawder and Lady Juliet standing together, talking to two gentlemen. Did his eyes deceive him, or were Miss Lawder's cheeks a little flushed? His eyes narrowed further, trying to make out each of the gentlemen. Was one of them Lord Wollaston? Recalling just how much interest the fellow had expressed in Miss Lawder, Giles felt a stone drop into the pit of his stomach. Despite Miss Lawder's protestations, he was quite sure that the gentleman could be most persuasive – and determined in his efforts, if he truly was interested in the lady.

And why should he not be? Miss Lawder is the daughter of a Baron. She has a respectable social standing and is of marriageable age. I am sure he would find her character quite lovely, should he have the opportunity to know her a little better.

"Lord Bargrave!"

Lady Winthrop's sharp exclamation caught his attention, and he immediately drew his eyes back towards her.

"You have paid very little attention to me these last few moments. I have been expressing my discontent and my sorrow at our parting and you have not heard a single word!"

Giles held up both hands, palms out towards her.

"I mean no offense, Lady Winthrop. The matter, as far as I am concerned, is closed. I regret that you feel such sorrow, but I will not be moved."

Lady Winthrop threw a glance over her shoulder, her gaze snagging on Miss Lawder and Lady Juliet.

"Once again, you are concerned with your niece." Her eyes grew cold, her chin lifting as a tight line pulled at her mouth. "Or is it that you see someone else who might interest you in place of me?"

It took Giles a moment to realize that she was speaking of Miss Lawder. Dread began to fill him as he shook his head, fearful now that carefully chosen words from Lady Winthrop to the ear of society could cause Miss Lawder a great deal of trouble.

"Do not permit your sorrow to make you speak unfairly of others. I am committed to my niece. That is all."

Lady Winthrop's jaw tightened, and she put both hands to her hips.

"I know the sort of gentleman you are. The companion may be entirely innocent, but your interest is not."

"I have no interest in her, I assure you." Taking a small step closer, he lowered his head slightly, dropping his voice a fraction. "Should you decide to speak ill of either me or the young lady who is companion to my niece, then you must be aware that there will be severe consequences to follow. We have shared many things, Lady Winthrop, and kept many secrets. Secrets that I am yet willing to keep."

The harsh anger left her eyes and her shoulders dropped as her hands fell to her sides. She did not say another word to him, did not state outright that she would say nothing of either himself or Miss Lawder to society. Instead, she turned and marched directly across the room, as though she wished to get as far away from him as possible.

CHAPTER NINE

*E*mma looked around her. The ballroom was utterly magnificent, decorated in gold and red trim throughout. There was a sea of faces, and though she looked hard, she could not make any of them out with any particular focus. The noise of so many guests was almost overwhelming, and it took Emma some minutes to become used to the din.

"This is an absolutely magnificent ball, is it not?"

Searchingly Lady Juliet's expression for a moment, Emma smiled softly and put one hand on her charge's arm.

"I am sure that your uncle will give you a ball of your own very soon. You know that he has been trying very hard to make amends for the poor beginning he made with us. I quite believe that he did not realize that a ball such as this would have been most appropriate."

Lady Juliet frowned.

"You think I am a little jealous?"

"I think it entirely understandable. This ball is, as you say, utterly magnificent in every way. Any young lady of the *ton* would be glad a have such a ball given in her honor."

Lady Juliet's eyes twinkled for a moment.

"Yourself included?"

Emma laughed, but did not hide the truth from Lady Juliet.

"Yes indeed. I am quite certain that I should have loved a ball given only for me. I count myself in that also."

Lord Bargrave cleared his throat, catching Emma's attention. Her skin prickled as she caught the look in his eyes, wondering if he had overheard her conversation with Lady Juliet. Would he think her foolish to have said such a thing?

He did not look at all pleased to be present. His eyebrows sat low over his eyes and his eyes themselves were a little hooded. His gaze did not rest on any one thing, but darted here and there, as if searching for a way to escape. Whether or not he had been close enough to hear her conversation, Emma was quite sure now that Lord Bargrave had paid very little attention to what had been said.

Something is troubling him. I just do not know what it is.

"We must greet our hosts. It is a little discomfiting to me that we have not done so as yet."

Such had been the crush of guests that, as yet, Emma, Lady Juliet, and Lord Bargrave had not greeted Lady Fullerton, Lord Fullerton or his daughter, Lady Sarah Ann. Now, however, there appeared to be a break in the throng and after a moment, Lord Bargrave beckoned for them both to follow him. Emma went at once, close behind Lord Bargrave.

"Good evening, Lord Fullerton. Lady Fullerton. Lady Sarah Ann."

Lord Bargrave bowed as he made his greeting, allowing Emma a few moments to observe the three people before her. Lord Fullerton was far older than his wife, just as she had expected. He was short and rotund with a balding head and a thick, grey mustache. He appeared, however, to be a kind sort, for his smile was wide and his eyes alive with evident happiness – and from the moment that Lord Bargrave finished his words of greeting, Lord Fullerton let out great expressions of delight at seeing both himself, Lady Juliet and Emma. Having been quite unused to such effusive displays, Emma found herself a little taken with Lord Fullerton.

"Thank you, Lord Fullerton. Might I introduce my niece, Lady Juliet Millwood, and her companion, Miss Lawder."

Lord Fullerton bowed.

"I am honored to make your acquaintance, Lady Juliet. And I am even more delighted that your companion - who is so young and so beautiful in her own right - has also been given leave to join us."

Emma's blush warmed her cheeks.

"You are very kind, Lord Fullerton. I am grateful to be included in such an invitation."

Lord Fullerton chuckled.

"I speak only the truth, my dear - as my wife and daughter well know."

He then gestured to Lady Fullerton and Lady Sarah Ann, who both smiled and curtsied, although Lady Fullerton's smile did nothing to brighten her eyes. Indeed, she appeared somewhat tight-lipped, and her gaze was not directed towards either Emma or Lady Juliet. Instead, it often lingered on Lord Bargrave, but only for a moment or two before flitting away again.

"I must hope, my dear Lord Bargrave, that you will consider dancing this evening?"

Lady Fullerton turned herself a little more towards him,

her smile somewhat fixed as she then gestured pointedly towards her daughter. Emma caught the slight start which ran down Lord Bargrave's frame – evidently, he was taken a little by surprise by such a direct question. He cleared his throat but did not hesitate.

"I should be delighted to do so, of course. It would be an honor to dance with the lady of the evening."

Emma allowed her gaze to linger on Lady Sarah Ann. She appeared a very fine young lady, who would be of an age with Lady Juliet, given that this was also her come out. She had fine brown eyes, but was not overly tall, perhaps gaining her stature from her father. Thus far, she had said very little and continually looked towards her stepmother as if waiting for confirmation of what she should say or do next.

"You shall have to *give* your dance card to my uncle, if you wish him to dance with you, Lady Sarah Ann!"

Lady Juliet laughed softly, but Lady Sarah Ann did not respond to this with a smile. To Emma's surprise, the young lady's face turned scarlet, her hands curled into fists, and she took a step forward as if to challenge Lady Juliet in some way. Emma's breath caught in her chest, her eyes fixed on the lady - this behavior was most concerning, and the change in Lady Sarah Ann's expression was a little frightening. Emma put a restraining hand on Lady Juliet's arm, glancing at her and seeing the smile slide from her face. It seemed that Lady Sarah Ann had not appreciated Lady Juliet's jesting.

"Forgive my niece." Lord Bargrave chuckled, although his eyes were a little darker blue when he threw them both a glance. "Lady Juliet can be inclined towards teasing – something which I have, unfortunately, had to become used to!" Putting a broad smile on his lips, he held out one hand towards Lady Sarah Ann. "Forgive me, I should have thought to ask you for such a thing. Allow me to do so now." Taking a pause, he inclined his head slightly. "Might I have your dance card, Lady Sarah Ann?"

It took Lady Sarah Ann some moments to respond, and when she did so, it was with tight, jerky movements.

"Of course, Lord Bargrave."

Lady Fullerton murmured the words, turning her head to pin her stepdaughter with sharp eyes. Lady Sarah Ann dropped her head, the color fading from her cheeks as she slipped the dance card from her wrist and held it out towards Lord Bargrave. Emma caught the way that Lady Fullerton reached to grasp Lady Sarah Ann's hand in her own, seeing the whiteness around the lady's knuckles. Evidently, she was aware that Lady Sarah Ann's behavior had been most concerning.

It did not take Lord Bargrave long to decide which dance he wanted, and within a few moments, they were ready to take their leave of the hosts.

"I do hope that you have a most enjoyable evening." Lord Fullerton smiled, as though there had been nothing amiss whatsoever. "And thank you for attending my daughter's ball. We are honored to have you here."

The moment that they walked away, Lady Juliet's hand went to Emma's arm.

"Good gracious! Whatever happened with Lady Sarah Ann?"

"I do not know." The back of her neck prickled as though she somehow knew that Lady Sarah Ann and Lady Fullerton were watching them walk away. "It was most extraordinary."

Lord Bargrave cleared his throat to catch their attention.

"I am quite certain that Lady Sarah Ann only behaved

so because she is a little overwhelmed by the evening. On any other occasion, I'm quite certain that she would have laughed or found mirth in your remark, Lady Juliet. It would be best for us not to consider the matter any further, else it may well spoil the remainder of the evening."

Emma bit her lip and looked away, wondering if there was something of a reprimand in Lord Bargrave's words.

"You need not fear, Uncle. I shall not speak ill of Lady Sarah Ann to anyone. I am not inclined towards gossip."

"For which I am very grateful," came the reply. Lord Bargrave smiled at Lady Juliet, which Emma caught as she glanced up at him. "Now, I fully expect that you will dance every dance this evening, Juliet, But I must beg of you to make certain that you step out with only the finest of gentlemen."

"And by that you mean me to avoid Lord Kincaid."

Lord Bargrave stopped, turned, and pressed one hand to his heart.

"I do. I want the very best for you, Juliet. Lord Kincaid is not a gentleman to be trusted, as I have made quite plain."

"Both myself and Miss Lawder have taken it to heart." Lady Juliet tilted her head towards Emma for a moment. "And if a gentleman should wish to dance with Miss Lawder? What should you say then?"

Emma's heart slammed hard in her chest, and she immediately shook her head.

"My dear Juliet, you need not even think of such a thing. My response is already quite clearly laid out in my mind."

Lady Juliet tutted.

"It seems most unfair that you will not stand up with a single gentleman simply because you are my companion. You are almost of an age with me, and you are a lady of society. There seems no reason why you should not behave just as you wish."

To Emma's surprise, the fervency in Lady Juliet's eyes was matched by her speech.

"There is no need for me to do so. I am perfectly contented in my role."

Seeming to forget about the other guests who were around her, as well as the fact that Lord Bargrave stood nearby, Lady Juliet shook her head, her fingers gripping Emma's arm tightly.

"We have become very dear friends. Ever since Lord Wollaston showed particular interest in you, I have begun to question whether or not you ought to be more than just my companion." One hand lifted in the direction of Lord Bargrave. "After all, I have an uncle here to act as my chaperone if needed."

Something like panic filled Emma's chest.

"Please, Juliet. This is not the time nor the place to have such a discussion. As I have said, I am more than contented in my role here at present. I have no wish for anything else."

"But will you be able to say such a thing in a few years?" Lady Juliet moved a little closer, her determination insistent. "*Now* is the time to grasp such an opportunity, *before* you are considered on the shelf. I know that your father thinks you nothing but a burden, but I think you are a good deal more than that. I think you worthy of the London Season. I think you worthy of a happy marriage. I think you worthy of a family of your own and to be called mistress of your own house."

Emma's mouth went dry as her heart twisted.

"I have spent a long time reminding myself that such opportunities are never to be mine." Lowering her voice, she pressed Lady Juliet's hand, wishing her to remain silent on the subject. "I will not pretend that such a thing is not painful, but I have endured it. I am more than contented in my situation. In fact, I consider myself fortunate indeed to have found such a charge as you."

Lady Juliet blinked rapidly, her eyes suddenly filling with unshed tears.

"I shall not have it." Her voice was hoarse, and she shook her head quickly, lowering it for a moment as she drew in a ragged breath. "If you do not seize this opportunity, then I fear that you will never find a happy situation for your future. You will always be either a companion or a governess or some other such thing, when by rights you ought to be a lady. I have no qualms about you behaving as such."

Emma swallowed against the tightness in her throat. If she were honest with herself, then she knew all too well just how much she desired to have everything that Lady Juliet had suggested. Yes, her father rejecting her had been incredibly painful and the future that he had laid out for her had been difficult to accept. But having resigned herself to the fact that there was nothing else for her but this, Emma had sought to find happiness and contentment in her situation. Pushing aside her own sorrows, she had focused entirely on Lady Juliet and wanted now to continue to do so, simply so that the pain in her heart would not envelope her completely.

"Alas, my dear Lady Juliet, you are not the one who has employed me." Speaking softly and ignoring the searing pain in her heart, Emma squeezed her friend's hand and then released it. "You are most kind, however."

Lady Juliet opened her mouth to say something only for Lord Bargrave to interrupt.

"Would you like to dance, Miss Lawder?"

The shock which poured into her had her feet fixed to the floor, her eyes wide and staring. Had she truly heard him ask her such a thing? Whatever was he thinking? An Earl could not ask a companion to dance! The entirety of the *ton* would see them stepping out together and the rumors around her presence in Lord Bargrave's house would spread like wildfire. Hearing Lady Juliet's exclamation jerked her back to the present, but she could not give Lord Bargrave an answer.

"I think that is an excellent idea!" Lady Juliet gave her a gentle nudge towards Lord Bargrave, but Emma immediately closed her eyes as a tremor ran through her frame. "The *ton* will see that you are an eligible young lady and–"

"But I am not!" Sharply interrupting Lady Juliet, Emma's eyes flew open just as the smile shattered on Lady Juliet's face. "I am not an eligible young lady. I have no dowry, I have no father nor brother here to present me. I am an employed person. I am here solely because it is my duty, rather than because I am free to attend society. You cannot present me as a potential match when I am not." Her shoulders dropped as tears came into her eyes. "You are very kind, Lady Juliet, and I greatly appreciate every favor you wish to push upon me, but I am not as you are. I can never be so." Her hands flung outwards for a moment before they fell to her sides again. "What sort of gentleman would truly consider someone such as me? Someone whose father has renounced her. Someone who has no dowry. It is a dream, Lady Juliet. Nothing but a dream."

Had it not been for the buzz of the crowd around them, there would have been nothing but silence between them all. Emma let her eyes drift to the floor, her heart aching still, though she kept as much of it as she could from her expression.

"Come with me, Miss Lawder."

Without warning, Lord Bargrave reached for her hand. Emma's breath was snatched away as he led her gently towards the dance floor before taking her in his arms in the waltz position.

"I... I do not think I have ever danced the waltz."

Her whole body felt numb as a knot tied itself in her stomach. Her eyes went to her hand, held warmly in Lord Bargrave's own, blinking rapidly as though she could not quite believe what she was seeing.

"You need not be concerned. I shall lead you."

Lord Bargrave was not looking at her, but rather kept his gaze just to her left. Emma licked her lips, her mind suddenly screaming with the shock of what he had done. Every muscle in her body began to tighten and she squeezed her eyes closed, in the faint hope that when she opened them, she would be standing beside Lady Juliet.

"You will need to look at me, however."

The hint of mirth in Lord Bargrave's voice made Emma's eyes flare. Her heart was beating so furiously that she was quite sure he was able to hear it. Everything in her begged her to step back, to step away, and to let Lord Bargrave release her - but at the very next moment the music began, and she was caught up in his arms, swept into movement. It was all Emma could do to cling to Lord Bargrave. She stumbled once and let out a small exclamation of embarrassment, but Lord Bargrave was unhindered.

"Look at me." His soft but determined words forced Emma's eyes towards his. "You are doing very well. Do not be so afraid. Hold fast to me, and all shall be well."

There was nothing else for Emma to do but to obey. Her hand clasping tightly in his, her other hand resting upon his shoulder, she kept her gaze fixed and allowed his steps to lead hers. The sea blue of his eyes seemed to shift like the rolling waves, vivid and strong - and Emma's heart roared in response.

She felt everything and nothing in one moment. Her heart ached, and yet a smile began to pull up the side of her mouth as though she were happy. She could not look away from him. There was no reasonable explanation for why he had done such a thing. But as the dance continued, Emma found herself slowly relaxing in his arms. The tension left her limbs, the stiffness removed itself from her shoulders And her smile slowly grew.

"You are an excellent dancer. Miss Lawder."

The music came to an end and Emma found herself released. It took her a moment to remember to curtsey, her face burning scarlet as she did so.

"I was always taught to dance. The dancing master came to teach my brother and I was included also. That was before my father decided to send me away." *Why am I telling him such things as this?* Trying to cover her embarrassment, Emma lifted her head and turned towards Lady Juliet. "I am only glad I did not embarrass you, Lord Bargrave."

"You did not embarrass me in the least."

Rather than walking beside her, back towards Lady Juliet, Lord Bargrave offered her his arm. Having no other choice but to accept, Emma placed her hand on it and they walked back together towards her charge - who was standing stock still with wide eyes and a gentle smile.

Emma's heart was beating furiously still, but she did all she could to ignore it. Forcing a smile to her lips and unable to catch Lord Bargrave's eye, she came to stand beside Lady Juliet.

"Goodness, I did not know you could dance so well."

Emma dropped her gaze.

"I was only telling Lord Bargrave that the dancing master –"

"It was not to you that I was referring." Interrupting her, Lady Juliet put one hand on Emma's arm. "Instead, I was speaking of my uncle."

Lord Bargrave said nothing. Instead, he merely smiled, bowed, and then excused himself, leaving Emma quite nonplussed. She was about to remark on how strange it was that he had left them alone, only for someone to speak Lady Juliet's name. turning. She saw two gentlemen bowing towards them and quickly realized that Lord Bargrave had absented himself so that they might talk to these gentlemen without his overbearing presence.

I still do not understand why he insisted that we dance together.

As the two gentlemen began to speak with, primarily, Lady Juliet, Emma was allowed a few moments to consider what had just taken place. Her heart was only now beginning to quiet down, whilst her mind began to fill with questions over what his motivations had been. Surely now a good number of the *ton* would notice what he had done and would speak of it amongst themselves - and what good would that do her? Had she not just finished telling him *and* Lady Juliet of her situation? Had she not promised him over and over that she was devoted to his niece? Why, then, had he taken her out to dance?

Her questions remained unanswered, however, and as the two gentlemen began to speak of dancing, Emma was pulled back to the present and her responsibilities. Her mind remained fixed upon Lord Bargrave, however, and despite her frustrations and her many inner questions, Emma could not pretend that his actions had not touched her heart. It could be that her dance with Lord Bargrave was the only one she would ever take part in - and what an amazing dance it had been! It was not one she was likely to ever forget. Lord Bargrave had shown her kindness and even though she had felt embarrassment and was still concerned about what complications might arise, there had been a great consideration on his part towards her - and for that Emma had to admit that she was immensely grateful.

CHAPTER TEN

In comparison to his dance with Miss Lawder, the dance with Lady Sarah Ann was an excruciating experience. Every time they took hands, she gripped his so tightly that it was a little painful, causing him to wince. He was then forced to hide that expression from both the lady, and from those watching, and instead gritted his teeth and forced a smile which he was quite certain looked like nothing of the sort.

Lady Sarah Ann was not a plain creature by any means, but there was something about the pinched expression which continually tore its way across her face that made her a little unappealing. It was as though everything and everyone were upsetting her in some way, as though she were keeping her silent discontent entirely to herself but permitting it to etch itself into her eyes and her mouth regardless. On more than one occasion, Giles was afraid that he had trodden on her toes or made a misstep, but he had quickly assured himself that he had done nothing of the sort. Perhaps, he considered, it was that she simply did not enjoy dancing with him - and that would be a good thing for it would mean that she would not hope to have him step out with her again.

It was with relief that Giles noted the music beginning to slow. When the dance came to an end, he was ready with his bow and did not have to wait long for Lady Sarah Ann to return it with a curtsey.

"I thank you for the dance, Lord Bargrave."

A brief smile flashed across Lady Sarah Ann's face, but it did not bring any joy or delight to her expression. Her dark eyes remained blank, and Giles could not help but think of Miss Lawder's hazel eyes, recalling how they glinted with gold whenever she chose to smile – which, to his mind, appeared to be very often in comparison with Lady Sarah Ann!

"But of course, Lady Sarah Ann."

Gesturing towards Lady Fullerton, who was talking with another lady in the corner of the room, Giles began to walk towards her, expecting Lady Sarah Ann to follow.

"You do not offer me your arm."

Turning back to face Lady Sarah Ann, Giles blinked in surprise. The young lady had gone very red in the face again, and her eyes were narrowed into slits. His gaze rested on both her hands, seeing how they were balled up tightly. Evidently, he had upset her greatly.

"But of course." Returning to her, he held out his arm at once, and Lady Sarah Ann accepted without hesitation, although her eyes remained narrowed as if she wished the entirety of the ballroom to see that she was displeased with him. "Forgive me, Lady Sarah Ann. Our acquaintance has not been of a long duration, and I did not think that such a thing would be agreeable to you."

"Then you are mistaken."

The sharpness of her tone sent shock ricocheting up,

Giles' spine, but he remained silent with an effort. After all, he reasoned, Lady Sarah Ann was irritated with him and given that this was a ball thrown in her honor, he did not want to do anything which would embarrass or upset her. In silence, they walked back towards Lady Fullerton, where Giles had to stop himself from practically shaking Lady Sarah Ann's arm from his.

"Thank you for dancing with me. It was most enjoyable."

Inclining his head Giles meet to take his leave, but Lady Fullerton reached out and grasped his arm with two delicate fingers and thumb.

"Wait a moment, if you please." Casting an eye towards her daughter, she then looked back towards Giles, who found himself shifting from foot to foot as his heart began to quicken. Whatever did she want with him? "It has been some time, has it not? I am sure that you were a little surprised by my presence in your house some days ago."

Giles took in a breath. This was not something he wished to discuss, and he certainly did not want to do so in the presence of Lady Sarah Ann.

"The past is forgotten. I am very grateful to you for your invitation, for I have had the very best of evenings, as I hope you also have done, Lady Sarah Ann." Inclining his head for a moment, Giles again made to take his leave, but Lady Fullerton did not appear to be finished with their conversation.

"Perhaps you might wish to call upon me at some point soon. You say that the past is forgotten, but there are some things which I should still like to say. Some apologies which must yet be made."

Whether it was from the sharpness in her eyes, or the uncomfortableness of the situation, Giles did not know. The only thing that he found himself doing was nodding as though he was eager to do as Lady Fullerton suggested when in truth he could not think of anything worse.

"Excellent. I am certain that my daughter will be very pleased indeed to see you... as shall I."

The smile which flitted across Lady Fullerton's face was so brief that Giles was not quite certain he had even seen it in the first place. The very next second, her expression returned to that cool, calm picture that hid so much and said so little. As he considered that expression, Lady Sarah-Ann spoke.

"Yes, I should be very glad to have you call upon me. Our dance has been my favorite thus far."

Alarm began to wind its way up Giles' chest and around his neck. Lady Fullerton had asked him to call so that she might make an apology for the past but, from what Lady Sarah Ann had said, it appeared that she believed that he would call simply to see her.

That is an idea I wish to remove from her mind immediately.

"That is very kind of you, Lady Sarah Ann, but I will call solely to speak to your stepmother for only a short while." His manner was a good deal more blunt than he would usually have exhibited, but Giles considered it merited, given the situation. "My sole consideration this Season is for my niece, Lady Juliet. I must make certain that she enjoys her first Season."

Lady Fullerton blinked, one eyebrow arching gently.

"You are not seeking a match for her, then?"

"Of course, but as I am certain that you are aware, one's first Season does not always lead to matrimony."

The sound of a sudden sharp intake of breath caught his attention and he turned his gaze back towards Lady Sarah

Ann. He was astonished at the way she stamped her foot, her eyes glaring back towards him as though he had caused her some great ill.

"That is preposterous! It should be the sole purpose of every young lady to make as good a match as they can, not merely to 'enjoy themselves', as you say. In fact, I think it quite ridiculous that you, an eligible gentleman, are not yet wed yourself!"

For what was the third time that evening, Giles found himself caught with such an astonishment over Lady Sarah Ann's behavior that, for a moment, he could not speak. Lady Sarah Ann's face was bright red, and her lips pulled into such a tight line that they were white at the corners.

"Sarah Ann, my dear, pray be silent."

Lady Fullerton's hand pressed Giles's arm.

"You understand, Lord Bargrave, that my stepdaughter is rather anxious this evening. She is allowing herself to say things which she would never say otherwise, such is her tension and strain." A laugh came from her lips, but it was forced and guttural, doing nothing to quell Giles' shock. "A ball thrown in one's honor may be a very fine thing indeed, but it can cause a great deal of distress as well. We shall not take up any more of your time. I look forward to speaking with you whenever you have the opportunity to call."

As she released his arm, Lady Fullerton gave him a gentle tug and Giles found himself turning away from Lady Sarah Ann altogether. He needed no further encouragement to depart from the lady's company - he strode quickly across the room in search of a glass of champagne.

"Was that Lady Sarah Ann I saw you speaking with?" Moving away from another conversation, Lord Berkshire came to join Giles as he drank his glass of champagne a little too quickly. "Goodness! Was the conversation truly so trying?"

Giles chuckled grimly and reached for another glass.

"You would be astonished if I were to tell you the truth."

Lord Berkshire grinned.

"Alas, I fear I already know it. You are not a gentleman inclined to listen to gossip and rumor - and under normal circumstances I myself would not be either. But my wife is much more inclined to listen and to pass these things on, and thus I am forced to pay heed."

A flicker of interest sent a line between Giles' eyebrows.

"You mean to say that certain things are being said of Lady Sarah Ann?"

A hiss of breath escaped from his friend as he nodded.

"Normally I would not pass such things on, but from the brief interactions I have had with the young lady, I must admit that these rumors appear to be true."

Giles rolled his eyes.

"If you are about to tell me that you find her rude and with a great temper for someone so small then yes, I shall agree with you wholeheartedly."

Lord Berkshire shook his head ruefully, a sigh breaking from his lips.

"My wife was a little upset. She made a very kind remark about Lady Sarah Ann's gown, and for whatever reason, the young lady took it as a slight."

"That is troubling."

"The rumors state that Lord Fullerton is unable to control his daughter. Lady Sarah Ann has a reputation for being cruel and unkind, to the point that they have not been able to keep a lady's maid for more than a few days!"

Giles grimaced.

"I presume Lord Fullerton's staff have been talking."

"No doubt, but it appears from Lady Sarah Ann's behavior this evening that the rumors certainly have a basis in fact. It is said that her temper is so ferocious that dinner plates have been thrown and ornaments smashed." Lord Berkshire's expression darkened. "I shall not place the blame solely upon Lord Fullerton's shoulders, but from what I have heard, he gives her everything and anything she *states* she requires. She gives not even the slightest consideration to her stepmother."

For a moment, sympathy rose in Giles's chest as he considered Lady Fullerton and all that she must now endure.

"I confess myself reluctant to spend any further time in Lady Sarah Ann's company. I would not have danced with her, had not Lady Fullerton asked me directly. But now, I have agreed to call upon Lady Fullerton, at some point in the future – It would not have been polite to refuse."

Lord Berkshire raised an eyebrow.

"Then you must either escape that obligation somehow or approach it with great caution. I believe that Lady Fullerton is doing all she can to make certain that this ball is a success. No doubt both she and her husband have heard of the rumors and do not want it to adversely affect Lady Sarah Ann's chances of making a suitable match."

"And thus, the reason for her direct question was to make certain that her stepdaughter has as many dances as possible." Understanding dawned and Giles ran one hand over his face. "It is a pity that Lord Fullerton has spoiled his daughter so. I do not think that she will do well this Season if she continues to display her temper in such a way." A scowl spread across his face. "I doubt she will ever make a suitable match."

"There may have to be cause for an arrangement. I am sure that Lord Fullerton has an excellent dowry for her."

"Even still." Giles shook his head, wincing at the thought. "Even *hearing* such rumors would put me away from ever considering Lady Sarah Ann in a marriageable light."

Something gleamed in Lord Berkshire's eye.

"Can I ask who, if anyone, you might then consider in such a light?"

Giles narrowed his eyes, seeing the twitching smile crossing his friend's lips.

"Do you have a reason for such a question?"

"Is it very often that a gentleman will stand up with a companion?"

A blossoming heat began to grow in Giles' chest, but he shook his head dismissively. The truth was that he was not yet quite certain why he had done such a thing, but now was not the time to consider it."

"There is nothing in that. She is my niece's companion. But I felt I was so obliged to her."

"Obliged?" Lord Berkshire's eyebrow lifted still farther. "Why should you feel obliged to your niece's companion. What is it that she requires of you?"

Giles smiled wryly.

"You and I have long been friends and I can always tell when you are attempting to garner something from me. I am afraid I shall not oblige you further in this regard."

Lord Berkshire shrugged but the twinkle in his eye remained.

"Surely you know that you need not pretend with me. If there something in your heart that you wish to share about the lady, then..."

"There is nothing."

Given that I am still rather confused over my actions towards her, I do not think I would have been able to share anything of importance with Lord Berkshire even if I had wished to.

"There is no shame in having particular feelings for a young lady... even if she is a companion."

"I do not think that I am particularly inclined towards 'feelings'." Giles smiled and tried to shrug off the remark, but Lord Berkshire only frowned. "Let us talk of something else." Finding that there was a slight strain between himself and his friend, Giles shook himself slightly and laughed. "This discussion of emotions and the like leaves me greatly disconcerted. Perhaps instead you may advise me as to how I ought to behave when it comes to Lady Sarah Ann."

"The only advice I can give is to make your interactions with her as short as possible!" Lord Berkshire grinned and immediately the tension between them shattered. "And certainly, say nothing which would upset her. In fact, it would be best if you said nothing at all!"

"Then, no doubt, she will be upset that I have given her no compliments," Giles complained as his friend chuckled. "I must admit that I am not looking forward to this occasion at all."

∼

"My mother informs me that you were once dear friends, Lord Bargrave."

Giles shot a quick look towards Lady Fullerton, but she remained precisely as she had always been, ever since he had arrived. She sat upright in her chair, a small but cold smile on her face. Her eyes remained fixed on her stepdaughter rather than looking towards Giles.

He cleared his throat.

"Yes, that is so."

"Before she wed my father, of course."

"Indeed."

Finding that there was very little else for him to say, Giles took a small sip of his tea. This visit had not gone as he had expected. Lady Fullerton had remained almost entirely silent while her stepdaughter had made most of the conversation. Having thought that he had expressed himself very clearly at the ball, Giles was a little put out. It could not be that Lady Fullerton sought to push him towards her stepdaughter, surely? Again, he felt the need to make himself quite plain.

"I do think that my ball has been the very best London has seen for some time. It was a most magnificent evening."

Lady Sarah Ann smiled, but sent a slightly lifted eyebrow in Giles' direction, evidently waiting for his agreement.

"I had a very enjoyable time, yes." He refrained from stating that it was the very best he had attended thus far, simply so that he would not speak a mistruth, and continued the conversation in a more direct manner. "I find my Season a little different this year, however. I am sure you must also do so, Lady Fullerton." Smiling genially, he waited until Lady Fullerton looked directly at him before he continued. "In previous Seasons I have had nothing to think of other than myself. Now, however, my time is taken up with my niece! I have given my old activities entirely and now think only of her."

Looking towards her stepdaughter, Lady Fullerton turned her eyes away from Giles.

"Yes, I suppose I would agree with you, Lord Bargrave."

Waiting for her to say something further to continue the

conversation, Giles found himself once more lingering in silence. This was most frustrating indeed. Lady Fullerton had begged for him to call, under the guise of making an apology, but now it seemed as though she had very little intention of doing anything of the sort. Her only purpose, it seemed, was to push his attention towards her stepdaughter - even though Giles thought he had made it quite clear that he had no interest in matrimony.

It is time for me to depart.

"Yes, I find myself quite busy with everything that Lady Juliet requires of me. I am glad it is she who is seeking a match rather than myself, for it appears to take a great deal of effort and time." Slapping both hands to his knees, Giles rose from his chair just as Lady Fullerton's eyes flew immediately to his. "So saying, I must take my leave. My niece requires me later this afternoon and I should not wish to be tardy."

Both Lady Fullerton and Lady Sarah Ann rose to their feet at once.

"I did not think that you would be leaving so soon." For the first time, a hint of color came into Lady Fullerton's cheeks. "That is much too short a visit. We have not even had the opportunity to talk!"

There has been plenty of opportunity, but you have chosen not to take it.

"Alas, as I have said, Lady Juliet requires my company this afternoon, and my first consideration must be to her. Good afternoon, Lady Fullerton." Turning he bowed towards Lady Sarah Ann. "Good afternoon to you also, Lady Sarah Ann."

When he lifted his head, Giles was not at all surprised to see the angry eyes of Lady Sarah Ann staring straight back at him. From what he had heard from Lord Berkshire, and with his previous yet short experience of Lady Sarah Ann's company, Giles had expected her to be angered by his sudden departure. Being entirely unwilling to wait for her to explode in fury, Giles threw her a smile and then made to exit the room.

"You cannot leave so soon!"

He was a little too late. Lady Sarah Ann's exclamation reached his ears just as he put one hand on the door.

"I am sorry to have to do so, but I have no choice. As I have said, I must return to my niece. Perhaps we will meet again this afternoon in Hyde Park, if you are taking a walk there?"

"We are not going to Hyde Park today! That is not at all suitable. Why can you not sit with us? I *insist* that you stay a little longer!"

Lady Sarah Ann took a step forward, but Lady Fullerton was there by her side in a moment, her hand reaching out to grasp Lady Sarah Ann's wrist.

"You see just how much your company is desired, Lord Bargrave." Lady Fullerton's smile did not reach her eyes and her shoulders lifted with an obvious tension. "Thank you for calling upon us today. I do hope that you will feel able to call again another time. Enjoy your afternoon in Hyde Park with your niece."

Forcing a smile, Giles inclined his head again and then left the room with as much haste as he could manage without appearing obvious. Relief poured into him as he strode away, glad to be free of Lady Sarah Ann and Lady Fullerton's company. Lady Sarah Ann was very much inclined towards temper, and Giles simply could not understand Lady Fullerton's behavior. Why had she asked him to call when her only reason for doing so appeared to be to push him towards her stepdaughter? That was not what she had said when she had spoken to him at the ball. Giles had been under the impression that she had wanted to apologize for past behavior, had wanted to make amends so that they might step forward with something other than disregard for each other, but despite having many opportunities to speak, Lady Fullerton had remained silent.

Climbing into his carriage, Giles knocked on the roof, letting out a long sigh of relief as it began to pull away. He would not call upon Lady Fullerton again, no matter how often she asked him. There could be no trust there now. Remaining as cold, distant acquaintances was more than enough for Giles, and he had no regret in leaving Lady Fullerton and Lady Sarah Ann behind.

CHAPTER ELEVEN

"What think you of these?"

Emma took one of the gloves that Lady Juliet held out to her. Studying them for a moment, she nodded.

"They seem very well made. Do you like the color?"

"I do." Lady Juliet tilted her head one way and then the other, her lips pursed. "There is also another pair that I favor, however, in a slightly darker color."

"I cannot make such a decision for you, nor would I wish to, given the cost!" Hearing Lady Juliet laugh, Emma smiled at her friend. "There is no need for us to make any haste. Take as much time as you wish. I am more than contented wandering around this beautiful shop."

"Thank you."

After setting a hand on Lady Juliet's arm for a moment, Emma left Lady Juliet to look at the gloves for a little longer, choosing herself to examine the many bonnets which were available to purchase. She had very little doubt that Lady Juliet would come away from the shop with more than just a pair of gloves, but this was a pleasant afternoon and neither of them were in any rush to return to the town house. This evening there was to be another ball, but it was not until later that evening - besides which, Emma assumed that Lady Juliet would wish to wear something to the ball that she had purchased today.

"That one is very lovely."

Murmuring to herself, Emma rubbed the silk ribbon between her fingers, smiling at the thought of wearing such an expensive bonnet out to Hyde Park. Juliet had a father who would pay for her many purchases. Emma had practically no father at all, for while he was still alive and well, he had no interest in her life whatsoever.

A bell tinkled, and Emma glanced towards the door, seeing two other ladies come into the shop. She was about to look away when she realized that one of them was Lady Fullerton... which meant that the young lady beside her, who was a little hidden from view, was none other than Lady Sarah Ann.

Her stomach twisted and she turned back towards the bonnet, having very little interest in talking to either woman. Lord Bargrave had told them both that Lady Sarah Ann was known to have something of a temper, and Emma prayed silently that there would be no display of such a temper in the shop itself. One advantage of being a companion was that she did not need to say anything to anyone unless Lady Juliet invited or asked her to do so. It took a few moments for the ladies to greet each other, but Emma kept her attention turned towards the bonnets, keeping her face turned away. No doubt Lady Fullerton and Lady Sarah Ann would be a good deal more comfortable if she were *not* to join the conversation, given that she was only a companion. After all, Lady Fullerton had not even wanted to include her in the invitation to her stepdaughter's ball!

"Your uncle left my presence very quickly, indeed, I must say."

Lady Sarah Ann's harsh tone reached Emma's ears and she grimaced. Lord Bargrave had called upon Lady Fullerton and Lady Sarah Ann some four days ago, but it seemed that Lady Sarah Ann's displeasure over his hasty departure still lingered. The gentleman had informed both Emma and his niece of the visit and Emma had not been at all surprised to hear of the eagerness with which he had departed.

"Alas, he was required to walk with me in Hyde Park."

A quick glance over her shoulder told Emma that Lady Juliet was smiling, despite her rather cold tone.

"Then he shall have to call again. I am not at all pleased."

Lady Juliet murmured something, and within a few moments Emma felt her charge's presence by her side.

"I had to excuse myself. Pray, let us go."

Emma nodded and they left without a word. It was not until they had walked for a few minutes that Lady Juliet let out a small exclamation of dismay.

"The gloves! I had thought to purchase them, but I did not. I set them on the counter where the milliner stood, but was then pulled into conversation by Lady Sarah Ann."

Emma blinked, then turned back towards the shop.

"Come, then. We can go back. There is still time."

Lady Juliet did not follow after her.

"No, I cannot." Chewing on her lip for a few moments, she shook her head. "Not when Lady Sarah Ann is still present."

A little confused, Emma turned to face her friend.

"I do not understand - you are not afraid of the lady, are you?"

"No, I am not at all afraid. I am only concerned about what I might say should I get into conversation with her again." A little embarrassed, Lady Juliet dropped her head forward, her eyes on the ground. "It took me a great deal of strength to keep my temper when she spoke so poorly of my uncle. That is why I asked to leave."

Despite the seriousness of the confession, Emma's lips twitched in a small smile.

"I suppose that I should congratulate you. I am aware that Lady Sarah Ann's presence can be very difficult to tolerate."

"Might you go and fetch them?" Lady Juliet looked back towards Emma with a hopeful smile on her lips. "They will, of course, need to be paid by my father."

Emma did not hesitate.

"But of course. I should not like to leave you long, however. Might we make our way to the carriage first and then I shall return once you are safely inside?"

Lady Juliet laughed and shook her head.

"The carriage is in sight. I shall be quite able to walk there alone." Reaching out, she squeezed her hand for a moment. "Although I am particularly grateful for your devotion to me. Thank you, Emma."

Smiling, Emma nodded, and then gestured for Lady Juliet to make her way back to the carriage. She did not turn back to the shop, however, until she saw Lady Juliet climb inside and the door close after her. Hoping that Lady Fullerton and Lady Sarah Ann had already left the shop. Emma made her way inside but found herself immediately disappointed. The two ladies were standing together, but their backs were turned towards her, which was something of a relief.

"Excuse me, I believe Lady Juliet wished to purchase a pair of gloves. Do you know which pair she was considering?"

The milliner smiled, nodded, and excused herself to go and fetch the pair which Lady Juliet had wished for, having set them aside in case the lady returned. Emma stood silently as she waited, hearing only a murmur of conversation from Lady Sarah Ann and Lady Fullerton.

"But Lord Bargrave is –"

"It will come right, I assure you. You need not go on, Sarah Ann." Despite her awareness that she ought not to be paying any attention to what was being said, Emma could not help but turn her head towards Lady Sarah Ann and Lady Fullerton. Why were they mentioning Lord Bargrave? Both ladies were still looking away and Emma turned her head back again, not wanting to be caught glancing over at them. "I have promised that you will not be without a husband. I fully intend to make certain that you will have the very best of gentlemen by your side."

Something cold ran down Emma's spine and she closed her eyes for a moment, listening intently now.

"And you believe that Lord Bargrave is the very best of gentlemen? Pah!" Lady Sarah Ann's disdain was more than obvious. "I think him rude and dull and unfriendly and –"

"That is because you are a selfish, spoiled child who does not know what is good for her. Lord Bargrave is an Earl. He has an excellent fortune and superb social standing, and you will do very well to have him as your husband."

Emma blinked in surprise. Whatever were they talking of? Lord Bargrave had never given even the smallest hint that he would consider marrying - and she certainly would have not believed him to have even *thought* of Lady Sarah Ann as a bride!

"The gloves, my lady."

Taking a deep breath, Emma tried to smile and quickly finished the transaction. Praying that Lady Fullerton and Lady Sarah Ann had not recognized her, she hurried from the shop and returned at once to the carriage where Lady Juliet was waiting.

"Thank you." Lady Juliet was effervescent in her gratitude. "I am so very appreciative." Taking the small packet from Emma. Lady Juliet glanced at her, then frowned. "Is something wrong?"

"I... I am not yet sure." Taking a deep breath, Emma set her shoulders and forced a smile. "It is nothing that concerns you. Come, now we must return home, for you are to have a new gown for the ball this evening, are you not?"

Lady Juliet nodded, but her eyes continued to search Emma's face.

"You would tell me if there were something severely troubling, I hope?"

Reaching across, Emma squeezed Lady Juliet's hand.

"Of course. Hurry now. Let us go home."

～

"Miss Lawder." Emma jumped as Lord Bargrave's deep voice came from the shadows. When she turned around, he was already stepping away from the books in the corner, walking towards her. "I apologize, I did not mean to startle you."

Emma's heart continued to race, even as the shock left her. Being alone with Lord Bargrave was making her hands clench tightly, as butterflies fluttered in her stomach. After their dance together a little over ten days ago, something had changed between them. Emma could feel it, and it was as though every time she looked into his eyes, they were back together in that moment. Her opinion of him had changed significantly these last few days. It was clear to her that Lord Bargrave was a gentleman of his word. His apology had been heartfelt, for he had made every effort to change his behavior thereafter. There was not even a hint of selfishness in any of his decisions and he clearly thought carefully about what Lady Juliet would require. Any accepted invitations had been chosen only because of what they might do for his niece. Whenever a particular gentleman has come to call, Lord Bargrave had always been present. Once the gentleman had departed, Lord Bargrave would give his niece his opinion of the man in question, letting her know whether or not he should be considered as a suitor. All in all, Emma found her opinion of Lord Bargrave to be very high indeed.

I just wish my heart would not tremble so in his presence.

"I assume my niece taking a little longer than usual to prepare herself for the evening."

Emma smiled up into his eyes.

"I am afraid that her ministrations will take a little longer, yes."

"Whereas you look more than lovely, Miss Lawder." She could not look away from him. His smile faded and his eyes darkened a little, as though he had only just realized what he had said. Her breathing quickened as he took a step closer, her tongue darting out to lick her lips. The nearness of him made her senses swim and she felt herself a little dizzy. "Tell me Miss Lawder, have I improved myself in your estimation?"

Nodding, Emma tried to smile in an attempt to cover all that she felt.

"But of course, my Lord. I can see how much you care for your niece."

"Perhaps there is something more I should do." Lord Bargrave frowned but looked away, his jaw suddenly tight. "I failed my niece at the beginning. I should like to make amends."

On instinct, Emma put a comforting hand on his arm for the briefest of moments.

"You need not continue to berate yourself. Lady Juliet is more than happy with her situation at present."

Her hand dropped back to her side, but Lord Bargrave suddenly reached out to catch her fingers. Again, his eyes held hers. Silence grew between them, and Emma felt as though every single part of her was screaming with anticipation - although quite what she was expecting she could not say.

"Miss Lawder, I think that I...." Lord Bargrave closed his eyes, shook his head, and dropped her hand. "Your opinion of me is of great importance. I am very glad to hear that you find me a little more tolerable."

"More than tolerable, I assure you."

Lord Bargrave twisted his head back towards her sharply and Emma's blush rose. She had meant her words as a compliment, but Lord Bargrave had clearly seen more meaning in them than that. Her mouth went dry, and she struggled to consider what next to say, uncertain as to these strange feelings which were beginning to rise within her.

I cannot care for Lord Bargrave! I cannot permit myself to think anything more of him than what he is to me – my charge's uncle and the Lord of this house.

A sudden recollection of Lord Bargrave and Lady Winthrop standing together shot back into her mind, and Emma dropped her head so that she would not have to look into his eyes any longer. Lord Bargrave already had an interest in a particular lady - perhaps he was pushing that aside for the moment so that he might concentrate solely on his niece... or the other consideration was that he was something of a rake who enjoyed sharing the warm company of many a lady. Either way, it was none of her business to know in which direction Lord Bargrave's interest lay. as she had told him herself. Her only duty was to Lady Juliet, and she would not allow herself to be distracted by anything... or anyone.

"Did... did you have an enjoyable afternoon?"

From the way that Lord Bargrave clasped his hands behind his back and shifted from foot to foot, Emma considered that he too must be struggling to think of what to say next. However, she was grateful for his question, for this was the subject she had wanted to discuss.

"Yes, we did, I thank you. Your niece was searching for a new pair of gloves."

Lord Bargrave lifted an eyebrow.

"And am I to expect the bill?"

Laughing softly, Emma shook her head.

"I believe the bill was directed to her father. You need not be concerned." Her smile faded slightly as she recalled what had occurred thereafter. "Lady Fullerton and Lady Sarah Ann came in to peruse the items in that shop at the same time. They greeted us, of course. However, Lady Juliet wished to depart soon afterwards, and I would not have returned to the shop had it not been for the fact that she left the pair of gloves behind."

Lord Bargrave chuckled.

"And am I now to pity you for being caught in conversation with them for the second time?"

Emma smiled briefly but shook her head. She had thought on this matter for the last few hours and had been rather quiet over dinner, wondering whether or not to tell Lord Bargrave of what she had heard. Silently, she was a little afraid that he would announce to her that he was considering marriage after all, and would not be surprised at her news about Lady Sarah Ann and Lady Fullerton's discussion. However, after considering it further, she had thought it best to be honest with him, no matter the consequences.

"They were in conversation, but only with each other. I did not wish to eavesdrop, but I could not help but listen when I heard them mention your name."

Lord Bargrave's eyes widened, and his smile fell from his lips in an instant.

"I beg your pardon? They were speaking of me?" He blinked but then waved one hand. "No doubt there were complaints voiced by Lady Sarah Ann about my recent visit. Seeing Lady Juliet would have brought that to mind."

"Yes…" Emma hesitated, then closed her eyes. It was easier to speak clearly when she was not looking at him. "There was mention of marriage, Lord Bargrave. I do not know if there is an arrangement between yourself and Lady Sarah Ann, but that certainly is what was being suggested. Forgive me if I have been foolish or if I have spoken out of turn, but I thought it best to inform you, in case this came as a surprise to you, as much as it did to me."

Her words came out in a rush, but relief poured into her heart as she finished speaking. Opening her eyes, she looked directly back into Lord Bargrave's face - and saw nothing but shock there.

It took him a few moments to respond, and when he did, his words were stammering and his face a little pale.

"I must tell you now, Miss Lawder, that there is no arrangement between myself and Lady Sarah Ann. I cannot quite believe that you even *heard* such a thing suggested!"

Not quite certain how she was meant to respond to this, Emma licked her lips and shrugged.

"You are a gentleman in good standing, my Lord. It is little wonder that some ladies of the *ton* think to consider you a suitable gentleman for their daughters."

Lord Bargrave let out a hoarse laugh but ran one hand down his face, evidently still overcome with surprise.

"That is very kind of you to say. However, I would beg of you to take no heed of such nonsense. I am not about to marry anyone – least of all Lady Sarah Ann!"

Emma pressed her lips together and nodded, dropping her gaze to the floor as she thought about what Lord Bargrave had said. He had no intention of marrying, therefore any thought she had of him, of drawing closer to him than she was at present, was nothing more than foolish whimsy on her part.

"I quite understand. Forgive me if I ought not to have said anything."

Lord Bargrave shook his head.

"You did no wrong. I am grateful that you have informed me of such a thing. In truth, I did wonder about Lady Fullerton's request for my visit. Now it seems that my suspicions were correct. I shall make sure to stay away from Lady Sarah Ann so that such an idea is quickly set aside."

"I do hope I have not embarrassed you."

"Embarrassed me? My dear lady, your consideration of me has touched my heart."

Striding across the floor, Lord Bargrave reached out

both hands as though to take hers, just for the library door to open and Lady Juliet to stand enthroned in the doorway.

"I *do* apologize for my tardiness. I simply could not decide which jewelry I was to wear."

Suddenly very aware of just how quickly her heart was beating and how the blood roared in her ears, Emma turned to face Lady Juliet directly, giving herself a slight shake as she did so.

"I think you have chosen very well."

"Thank you. And thank you again for going back to fetch the gloves. I think they make the perfect accompaniment to my gown."

"I shall agree with you there! But I shall state that I am glad that your father is the one paying the bill rather than I!"

Chuckling, Lord Bargrave stepped forward, leaving the conversation he had shared with Emma behind.

Emma followed them, seeing now that the matter was entirely closed. Glad that she had told Lord Bargrave what she had overheard, she found her heart still a little sorrowful. Lord Bargrave's declaration that he was not even considering matrimony had injured her in a way she had not expected.

That is because I am foolish.

Lifting her chin, Emma sent determination into her heart. She would not allow herself to become distracted by what she admitted she now felt for Lord Bargrave. Yes, she had come to care for him. Yes, she considered him a most excellent gentleman, despite their poor beginning - but she could never permit herself to be free with such emotions. It was naught but a fantasy; a dream of a gentleman and a companion - and such dreams, Emma knew, never truly came to be.

CHAPTER TWELVE

The moment Giles laid eyes on Lady Fullerton and Lady Sarah Ann, he turned around so sharply that he knocked into another gentleman who was accompanying a lady towards the dancing. Apologizing profusely, he continued to walk across the ballroom, making certain to set as much distance between himself and Lady Fullerton as he could.

The shock of what Miss Lawder had told him had still not worn off entirely - the buzz in his veins and the tightness in his chest told him so. At least now he could understand the reason for Lady Fullerton's request for him to call. She was just as manipulative and coercive as ever, it seemed, for she had promised to apologize, but instead had used the opportunity to encourage his attention to her stepdaughter.

"If you look like that for the rest of the evening, I can guarantee that you will have no one to dance with."

Lord Berkshire grabbed his arm just as Giles was about to walk out into the gardens.

"Are you planning to leave the ball already?"

Giles shook his head but did not smile.

"I should much prefer to be in White's, but I have my niece to consider."

The smile slipped from Lord Berkshire's face.

"Whatever is the matter?"

Taking a deep breath, Giles quickly explained and saw the frown begin to grow in his friend's expression.

"Goodness. You must be very grateful indeed to have such a person as Miss Lawder in your household. After all, she did not even need to tell you such a thing! She could have remained quite silent and allowed your personal matters to remain your own."

Giles had not thought of that. A wave of gratitude suddenly overwhelmed him.

"She appeared rather embarrassed to inform me of what she had heard. No doubt she did not wish me to think poorly of her for eavesdropping."

A sudden eagerness to make his way to the lady's side began to fill him and he looked over his shoulder as though she might be standing just behind him.

"I have also heard that Lady Winthrop is looking for another... warm acquaintance." A flicker of curiosity came into Lord Berkshire's eyes. "I thought you and she had something of an understanding."

A little embarrassed, Giles dropped his head. Running one hand over his chin, he shrugged one shoulder.

"That has come to an end. I did not feel the need to continue such an acquaintance this Season." This, however, sparked only further interest in Lord Berkshire's expression, making Giles's groan inwardly. "And no, I do not wish to discuss it further, before you ask," he stated, pre-empting his friend's questions. His smile suddenly grew as mischief came into his mind. "For a gentleman who supposedly does not like rumor and gossip, but who is forced to listen to it for the sake of his wife, you appear to be very interested in what is happening to me."

Lord Berkshire rolled his eyes and was about to say something when his eyes suddenly flared, and he looked sharply to one side. Giles, not fully understanding what his friend meant, was about to turn around when he heard none other than Lady Sarah Ann's high-pitched voice.

"There you are, Lord Bargrave, I have been looking everywhere for you. I do hope that you have not been deliberately avoiding me."

Giles widened his eyes in the direction of Lord Berkshire, but his friend merely shrugged and looked away. Afraid of what was to come should he give Lady Sarah Ann too much of his time, Giles quickly looked around in an attempt to find an excuse to soon depart from her company. The only person he could see, however, was Miss Lawder, standing next to Lady Juliet as she laughed and talked with two gentlemen and a lady. She did not look over. He had no choice but to engage with Lady Sarah Ann.

"Lady Sarah Ann." Bowing stiffly, Giles lifted an eyebrow. "You are come to talk to me... alone."

Surprised at the absence of both Lady and Lord Fullerton, Giles conveyed his astonishment in his expression. Lady Sarah Ann, however, did not seem to care, for she laughed and waved a hand as though he were being quite ridiculous.

"My stepmother will soon find me, I am sure. In the meantime, perhaps you might like to peruse my dance card? I only have one dance remaining, and it is the quadrille which is happening very soon." Her eyes glinted invitingly, and she held out her dance card to him. "I have saved this particular dance for you, Lord Bargrave. It is not the waltz, unfortunately, for that was already given to another, but the quadrille will do very well."

Frustration grabbed Giles's heart and he shook his head.

"I am afraid I cannot, Lady Sarah Ann, for I am already promised to dance the quadrille with another."

This, of course, was a total fabrication, for Giles had not offered to dance with anyone as yet. Lady Sarah Ann seemed to be aware of this also, for she narrowed her eyes, took a step forward and held her dance card out to him again.

"How can that be? You have spoken to none but this gentleman since you arrived."

Her hand flung out in the direction of Lord Berkshire but other than that, she did not acknowledge him.

Growing a little desperate, Giles threw a glance towards Lord Berkshire, but his friend's eyes flared in answer to his silent question. Lady Berkshire must already be engaged for the dance.

"Yes, that is so, but I have already arranged to dance with...." In his desperation, his mind fell to the only person he knew would be able to solve his dilemma. "...to dance with Miss Lawder." Relief poured into him as Lady Sarah Ann frowned, her hand dropping to her side. "I am to dance with my niece also of course, but the quadrille comes first."

Lady Sarah Ann's eyes narrowed.

"It is ridiculous that a companion should stand up with a gentleman when there are ladies present."

I find Lady Sarah Ann more dislikable with every minute that passes.

Before Giles could say anything, however, Lady Sarah Ann spoke again.

"I shall go and speak to her."

Shock flared in Giles' heart.

"I... I do not think that is at all necessary. The arrangement has already been made."

"It can be unmade. A companion should not stand in the way of a lady."

With a toss of her head, Lady Sarah Ann strode away from Giles and across the room towards Miss Lawder. Giles could only watch, horrified by the lady's arrogance and audacity. Miss Lawder, of course, knew nothing of such an arrangement, for it had been entirely made up to save him from dancing with Lady Sarah Ann.

"From your expression. I assume that this arrangement was of your own devising.?"

Lord Berkshire came to stand a little closer to Giles as they watched Lady Sarah Ann approach Miss Lawder.

"Yes, entirely." Giles groaned aloud, pinching the bridge of his nose. "It appears that I will have to dance with Lady Sarah Ann regardless."

"I would not be entirely convinced of that." Lord Berkshire gestured his chin towards where the two ladies spoke.

As Giles watched, he saw Lady Juliet approach as Miss Lawder shook her head. Perhaps the lady would save him after all.

His delight was short-lived as Lady Sarah Ann delivered a resounding slap to Miss Lawder's cheek. The sound seemed to echo around the ballroom and Giles' caught his breath, appalled at what the lady had done. His first instinct was to rush across the room towards them, but Lord Berkshire put one hand on his arm, holding him back.

"If you do that, then you will draw even more attention."

"But I must. Her honor has been compromised!"

Lord Berkshire's fingers tightened.

"Did you not complain to me some weeks ago about

Miss Lawder's fierce determination? Did you not state that you found her a little too sure of herself?" Gesturing towards Miss Lawder with his other hand, Lord Berkshire let out a dry cough. "I do not think you need have any concern. She is more than able to defend herself."

As Giles watched, both Miss Lawder and Lady Juliet stepped a little closer to Lady Sarah Ann and began to speak directly to her. A small smile crept across his lips as he saw how they both gesticulated and Lady Sarah Ann herself was forced to take a step back. He did not think that she would have expected such a reaction from a companion.

"Look, now she is coming over towards you."

Feeling Lord Berkshire's gentle nudge in his side, Giles could not help a smile as he saw Miss Lawder approaching. Lady Juliet was by her side and Giles felt a small swell of pride. Miss Lawder had not buckled in the face of Lady Sarah Ann's fury, and Lady Juliet had remained by her side, steadfast in her determination to reject the harsh cruelty of Lady Sarah Ann.

His smile broke as he saw the red stain spreading across Miss Lawder's face.

"I am so very sorry, Miss Lawder."

She gave him a small smile.

"It was hardly your doing, Lord Bargrave."

Giles winced.

"I fear that you are mistaken. Had I not told Lady Sarah Ann of our supposed dance, then she would never have gone to speak with you."

Miss Lawder smiled at him, her hazel eyes bright with shimmers of gold despite the redness in her face.

"You told Lady Sarah Ann that we are to dance together?"

"I did." A little embarrassed, Giles shook his head. "It

appears that Lady Sarah Ann has been watching me. She had only one dance remaining and knew that I had not promised it to anyone else since I had only spoken with Lord Berkshire since my arrival." Shrugging one shoulder, he spread his hands. "I presumed Lady Juliet's dance card would already be filled. I had no other thought but to turn to you."

"I quite understand, and I am very glad that you felt able to do so."

Lady Juliet smiled wryly.

"It is just as well you did, uncle, for my dance card is very nearly full and the quadrille is taken by Lord Taylor."

Giles allowed himself a small smile.

"I must make certain to dance with you also, however, so I will take whatever dance you have remaining! I stated to Lady Sarah Ann that I was to dance with both of you."

His niece laughed and pulled her dance card from her wrist before handing it to him.

"You may have the polka. I believe that is all that is left."

Giles quickly scribbled his name down, all the while glancing towards Miss Lawder. She was no longer looking at him but had ducked her head a little and was biting her lip. Perhaps the pain of Lady Sarah Ann's slap was finally making itself known.

"Oh, the quadrille has begun! Uncle, you must make haste."

Alarm shot through Giles's chest, but Miss Lawder shook her head.

"You need not stand up with me, Lord Bargrave. I quite understand if you said such a thing simply to make your excuses to Lady Sarah Ann."

Was this what concerned her? Did she truly believe that

he would not dance with her after what she had endured for his sake?

"I should very much like to dance with you, Miss Lawder." Her head lifted, a flash of light coming into her eyes. "That is, if *you* should like to dance with me."

Miss Lawder smiled.

"I should like that very much, Lord Bargrave."

Smiling, and with a heart filled with relief, Giles held out his arm to her and, after a moment, she took it.

"Come then, Miss Lawder. Let us go and dance together again."

CHAPTER THIRTEEN

"I believe your cheek is a little bruised. It certainly appears a touch swollen." Anxious eyes looked into her face, but Emma merely smiled. "Does it still pain you?"

Emma shook her head.

"Please, do not concern yourself. I pressed a cool compress to it earlier this morning."

Yesterday evening had been something of a whirlwind. When Lady Sarah Ann had demanded that she give up her dance with Lord Bargrave, it had taken Emma a moment to realize what had happened. A glance towards Lord Bargrave had told her of his desperation. Evidently, he had used her as an excuse so that he would not have to dance with Lady Sarah Ann, and Emma could not blame him for that. She had been upset at Lady Sarah Ann's arrogance, and frustrated by her selfishness, and thus had completely refused to give Lady Sarah Ann what she wanted. This has been seen as an affront, of course, and a slap across her cheek had been delivered.

Humiliation had threatened to overwhelm her, but

Emma had refused to give in to such an emotion. With Lady Juliet by her side, she had sent Lady Sarah Ann away with angry words following after her. The shock of Lady Sarah Ann's action had not sunk in until a few minutes later. All too soon, Emma had realized that many of the guests would have seen what had taken place – and thereafter, that Lord Bargrave danced with a companion rather than a lady. Afraid of the rumors and the gossip which would follow such an action, Emma had told herself not to hope that Lord Bargrave would *actually* dance with her. She had told herself not to hope, to hold no expectations - but then Lord Bargrave had proven himself to her once more. Joy had lifted her heart and she had forgotten about the pain in her cheek and the worry of rumors and gossip and even of Lady Sarah Ann. For a few minutes, she had been in Lord Bargrave's arms and nothing else had mattered.

"I would ask you what you are smiling about, but I do not think you would tell me even if I should do so."

Emma quickly dropped the smile from her face and turned her eyes towards Lady Juliet, who was looking at her with a slightly knowing smile on her lips.

"I do not know what you mean. I was thinking only of Lady Sarah Ann and all that occurred yesterday evening."

"And that made you smile so?" Lady Juliet's eyebrow lifted. "That does not seem quite right to me."

Emma shook her head but remained silent. It was not as though she could express to her charge exactly what it was that she felt for Lord Bargrave - after all, the gentleman was Lady Juliet's uncle! And in addition, Emma was not quite sure that Lady Juliet would keep her secrets. There was the risk that Lady Juliet might think the idea so wonderful that she would be unable to keep the news to herself.

"Very well, I shall not ask you anything further." Taking a deep breath, Lady Juliet smiled and reached across to squeeze Emma's hand for a moment. "We have an afternoon soiree to attend very soon. What if Lord Wollaston is there? I know he has been a little absent of late, but that does not mean that you need give up hope!"

Laughing softly, Emma shook her head, knowing full well that by saying such a thing about Lord Wollaston, Lady Juliet was attempting to garner a little more information from Emma as regarded her consideration of Lord Bargrave.

"I believe that Lord Wollaston is a gentleman who likes to say a good many things, but does not often follow through thereafter. I am quite certain that another young lady has caught his eye, and I feel no sorrow over that."

Lady Juliet arched one eyebrow.

"And why do you not?"

"Because I am a companion and as I have told him, I am more than settled with my lot. Hurry now, you must go and begin your preparations for this afternoon. We are to leave within the hour."

Lady Juliet rolled her eyes, laughed, and then rose from her chair, just as Lord Bargrave entered the room. A faint blush caught Emma's cheeks as she hurriedly got to her feet, meaning to follow Lady Juliet at once.

"I am just now going to prepare myself for the soiree, uncle." Lady Juliet smiled up at him as Lord Bargrave walked a little further into the room. "I do believe that you are quite prepared already, Miss Lawder. You need not come with me. I will return presently."

There was nothing for Emma to do but resume her seat, aware of the heat in her face and the tension now rippling through her frame. It was quite ridiculous for her to have so much affection in her heart for Lord Bargrave, but she could not help how she felt. Admitting it to herself was one thing, but acting upon it was quite another, and Emma had no intention of doing anything of the sort.

"How are you this afternoon? I apologize that I did not meet you for breakfast, but I had some business matters to deal with this morning."

His eyes roved over her face and Emma dropped her gaze, feeling the warmth in her cheeks burn all the more.

"I am quite well, I thank you."

"Lady Sarah Ann ought to apologize for what she did."

Emma's eyes flew to his, alarm suddenly growing in her chest.

"No, my Lord, pray do not demand such a thing. I am sure that the gossip around what occurred has already grown significantly, and I would not like to add to it."

Lord Bargrave's lips twisted and pulled to one side, annoyance burning in his expression. He remained silent for some moments, as though considering what she had said, and Emma's hand twisted together, waiting for him to respond.

"It does not sit well with me, Miss Lawder. You were dealt a great injury and Lady Sarah Ann's behavior was utterly unacceptable. I am a little shocked that you have not yet received an apology from the lady! I would have thought better of Lord Fullerton than that."

Giving him a small smile as relief burned in her heart, Emma spread her hands.

"Given my standing in society, I suppose they might consider that an apology is not required."

Lord Bargrave suddenly got to his feet, his face slowly turning a little pink.

"That should not have any bearing! I have a good mind

to march across to their house this very minute and demand it from them."

Emma found herself on her feet as Lord Bargrave came towards her, her hands reaching out to grasp his. At her touch, Lord Bargrave seemed to still, for his eyes went wide and his breath hitched, his hands suddenly tight on hers.

"Your consideration of me is most touching, my Lord." Despite the sudden tightness in her throat, Emma spoke with determination. "But you need not take any action. It is forgotten already, and I shall not personally make any demands for an apology from Lady Sarah Ann. Although," she finished, giving him a quick smile, "I shall endeavor to remain far from the lady from now on!"

Lord Bargrave smiled.

"We are in absolute agreement on that point! I thank you again for saving me from that particular situation last evening and I am sorry that you endured consequences which ought not to be on your head."

"It is quite all right."

A tap came at the door before they could say anything further, and Emma and Lord Bargrave's conversation came to an end. Smiling to herself, Emma resumed her seat as Lord Bargrave excused himself to deal with a small matter which had now been brought to his attention. In the silence which followed, she found herself letting out a small, contented sigh. She did not think that she had ever felt such a happiness as this.

∼

"It is as I feared."

Emma's eyes widened as she looked up at Lady Juliet.

"Whatever do you mean?"

Her charge's expression was a dark one. Lady Juliet's eyes were heavy with anger, and her brows low over them. Her jaw was tight, and no smile plucked at her lips. Alarm rose in Emma's heart.

"We shall have to take great care this afternoon. Lady Sarah Ann and her stepmother have just arrived."

Glancing over her shoulder, Emma saw the women standing together by the host and hostess.

"We need not be in the same room as they. Perhaps you would like a turn about the garden, or mayhap we should make our way to the library?"

"Perhaps the gardens?" Lady Juliet linked arms with Emma, and they began to make their way across the drawing room. "Did you have a good discussion with my uncle?"

It took Emma a moment to recall what Lady Juliet was referring to, only for her then to laugh softly.

"We talked only of last evening and, in particular, of Lady Sarah Ann." Seeing the disappointment in Lady Juliet's face, Emma shook her head. "Pray, do not begin to think that there is more to my relationship with your uncle than there is."

"But I am certain that he cares for you!" Lady Juliet exclaimed, making Emma immediately shush her. "I have seen how he watches you." Her voice was lower now, but her words sent spiraling heat into Emma's chest despite the cool breeze which came with stepping out of doors. "You make him smile more than any other person of his acquaintance."

"Hush now. Look, there is Lord Winchester. I am sure he will want to speak with you."

The gentleman immediately came over to Lady Juliet, as though he had known exactly what Emma had said.

Within a few moments, he and Lady Juliet were in conversation and Emma stepped back a little, allowing them to speak with a little more privacy.

The gardens were small but rather pretty. When Lord Winchester offered to walk with Lady Juliet for a short while around the garden, she agreed with a nod of approval from Emma. Still making sure to keep a short distance between herself and her charge, Emma clasped her hands behind her back and walked slowly after them. Moments later, another voice reached her.

"I am to write an apology."

Glancing back over her shoulder, Emma saw with dismay that Lady Sarah Ann was also in the gardens. She was walking with another young lady that Emma did not know, and her expression was pulled into the usual moue of distaste.

"That is *most* unfair!"

"I am well aware of that, but my stepmother is most insistent," came Lady Sarah Ann's reply to her friend's exclamation. "Normally, I would outright refuse, but there is a reason for her determination."

The two young ladies passed Emma and neither of them gave her even the smallest notice - and despite her requirement to remain with Lady Juliet, Emma could not help but follow them for a few moments – she could still see Lady Juliet, so surely, that was acceptable? If Lady Sarah Ann was to write an apology, what other reason would there be than to say that she was sorry? Given what Lady Fullerton had already tried to do, Emma could not help but be concerned.

"And what is such a reason? I confess that I am surprised that you would be willing to do something you have no wish to do."

Lady Sarah Ann threw her head back and laughed as though her friend had made the most ridiculous remark.

"Normally you would be correct - but once I had it all explained to me, I found myself *more* than willing."

A knot of fear tied itself in Emma's stomach. What was this reason? What other purpose could there be, other than to apologize?

She had no other time to listen, for Lady Juliet and Lord Winchester turned back and she was required to return to her charge at once. Or appear to be most inappropriate.

"Perhaps we should go back inside?" Lady Juliet cast a quick glance towards Lady Sarah Ann and threw Emma a wry smile. "I am a little chilled, now."

Lord Winchester seemed all too happy to accompany Lady Juliet back indoors and thus, Emma was pulled away from Lady Sarah Ann and her ongoing conversation. Her mind remained heavy with thoughts about what Lady Sarah Ann could have meant by her words. Confusion built in Emma's mind, and she shook her head to herself, wondering what it was that the lady had meant by such a thing.

Whatever the purpose was, Emma was well aware now that she would have to be cautious. Any apology, any letter which arrived for her, would quickly be read, and then considered at length. Any requests for meetings would be disregarded, for Emma did not trust either Lady Sarah Ann or Lady Fullerton. She considered them both dangerous and of equal concern to her. Lifting her chin, Emma allowed a tiny smile to pull at one side of her mouth. She had been fortunate indeed to overhear Lady Sarah Ann's conversation for now, at least, she could be on her guard.

CHAPTER FOURTEEN

"Where is your uncle?"

Emma frowned, glancing over at Lady Juliet as concern began to grow steadily in her heart. The three of them had eaten together, with the ladies taking tea in the drawing-room thereafter whilst Lord Bargrave drank his port and read over some papers. Once they had finished, Lady Juliet and Emma had retired to their rooms so that they might prepare themselves for the evening, but upon returning to the drawing-room, they discovered that Lord Bargrave was not waiting, as they had expected.

"I do not know."

Lady Juliet's frown matched Emma's. Walking across the room, she made to pull the bell, only for the door to open and the butler to enter.

"Lady Juliet, your uncle has asked me to inform you that he will be absent for a short while. He begs you to go to the ball with Miss Lawder, who will continue as your companion and your chaperone until he arrives."

"My uncle has left the house?" Surprise etched itself

onto Lady Juliet's expression. "At such a late hour? We were about to make our way to the ball together."

She exchanged a glance with Emma, who bit her lip with concern.

"Is there any reason to be concerned over Lord Bargrave's sudden absence?"

Stepping a little closer to Lady Juliet, Emma watched the butler shake his head.

"Then why did he leave the house so suddenly?"

The butler spread his hands.

"He received a letter, My Lady. I know not what was contained in it, of course."

A sudden fear clutched at Emma's heart.

"Do you know who the letter was from?"

The butler cleared his throat again and looked away, a slight redness coming into his face.

"It is not the place of a servant to know such particulars."

"Be that as it may, we must know whether or not you were aware of who had sent the letter." Emma stepped forward, recalling what she had overheard from Lady Sarah Ann earlier that day. "Tell us at once."

Lady Juliet's eyes widened in surprise, but she did not stop Emma. When the butler glanced towards her, Lady Juliet gestured for him to speak openly.

"I believe... I believe the seal was that of Lord Fullerton."

With her breath tightening in her chest, Emma turned directly back towards Lady Juliet, her eyes wide.

"I have made a mistake."

Lady Juliet waved one hand at the butler to dismiss him, then moved closer to Emma.

"I do not understand. What mistake are you speaking of? Do you not wish to go to the ball without him?"

Emma shook her head, panic beginning to clutch at her heart.

"Earlier today I overheard Lady Sarah Ann's conversation with another young lady. She was stating that her stepmother was insisting on an apology, and while she had no wish to do it, there was a strong purpose behind it."

"But why should that concern you? An apology is an excellent thing, is it not?"

"That is not what I mean." Shaking her head, Emma pressed one hand to her forehead, trying to calm herself enough to explain. "I believed that such an apology would come to my door, but due to the fact I am a companion, there would be some other reason behind that apology – perhaps an opportunity to smear me further rather than a genuine letter of contrition."

Understanding widened Lady Juliet's eyes.

"But the letter you were expecting has gone to my uncle."

"And now he has gone to Lord Fullerton's house. I do not know what was said within the letter, but there was something contained within it which required his immediate presence there." Briefly, she told Lady Juliet what she had overheard in the shop some days ago, seeing how Lady Juliet's eyes widened all the more as she spoke. "And now I am afraid that Lady Fullerton is about to enact some sort of plan to make certain that Lord Bargrave is forced to marry her stepdaughter."

Lady Juliet pressed one hand to her mouth, her eyes fixed on Emma's.

"But for what purpose?" she rasped, her hand falling to her side. "What reason could there be–"

"There is no time to ask such questions. We must go after Lord Bargrave at once before it is too late."

Urgency pushed Emma's steps as she hurried towards the door.

"Come, Lady Juliet. The carriage will be waiting."

Lady Juliet nodded and followed her, wringing her hands as she went. Within a few minutes the ladies were in the carriage, directing it towards Lord Fullerton's home. Emma's heart beat frantically, her fears mounting with every second.

If only I had realized that such a letter would not be sent to me!

Lady Fullerton and Lady Sarah Ann had barely given her a single moment's notice. Why then, would they send such a letter to her? It made sense that they would, instead, send an apology to Lord Bargrave directly. Whatever they had written in that letter had caused him to make his way to their home immediately. He did not know that he might well be walking into a trap.

"What do you intend to do? We cannot simply barge our way into Lord Fullerton's home!"

"Yes, we can." Emma gripped Lady Juliet's hand, a fierce determination burning in her heart. "If we do not, then I fear what will happen to your uncle. He may emerge from the house a betrothed gentleman."

The carriage came to a stop just in front of Lord Fullerton's house. Emma heard Lady Juliet's swift intake of breath but saw how her jaw tightened.

"What shall we say?"

The carriage door opened, and Emma stepped out into the cool evening air. Drawing in a deep breath, she set her shoulders.

"We shall ask the butler whether Lord Bargrave has

arrived. *You* will tell him that we need to speak with him at once, on a most urgent matter. Given that you are Lord Bargrave's niece, I do not think that the butler will refuse you."

Lady Juliet nodded.

"But if he should do?"

"Then we must make our way through the house directly until we find him. I know at the beginning Lord Bargrave did not think much of your direct manner nor my forwardness - but they may now be exactly what will save him."

Squeezing Lady Juliet's hand, Emma gestured toward the house. After a moment, Lady Juliet climbed the stone steps with Emma following, as was her place. The door was opened for them, and they stepped inside without hesitation.

"My uncle, Lord Bargrave, is here." Lady Juliet's voice rang around the hallway. "Bring him to me at once. Something terrible has happened and I must speak to him immediately."

Emma watched the butler closely, seeing how the man's eyes narrowed just a little. He clasped his hands behind his back but did not move.

"I am afraid I cannot. The gentleman is not here."

"You must be mistaken. Perhaps you were not standing at the door when he entered only a few moments ago. He was seen, you see."

The mistruth fell easily from Emma's lips, but it was enough to silence any further lies from the butler. He shifted slightly from one foot to the next, but then shook his head.

"I am afraid I cannot. I have been told not to disturb the mistress, not under any circumstances."

"That is ridiculous." Lady Juliet drew herself up to her full height, her hands going to her hips. "I am his niece. I demand to see him at once!"

The butler pressed his lips together until they were white. Evidently, his loyalty to his mistress overruled anything that Lady Juliet demanded. Emma's heart slammed hard against her ribs, and she sucked in a breath.

"Come."

Grasping Lady Juliet's hand, she tugged her away from the front door and into the house. immediately the butler began to protest, but Emma ignored him easily. She had very little idea of where she was going, pushing open one door and then the next.

"I really must protest. If you continue to do this, then I will have the footman –"

"What will you do?" Rounding on the butler, Lady Juliet poked one finger into his chest. "Shall you have them remove me bodily? Believe me, the scandal that would fall on this house thereafter would be great, particularly given that I have demanded to see my uncle as a matter of urgency, and you have refused."

The butler shrank back, and Emma hurried forward. She had very little idea which room was which, but she tried the next doorhandle regardless. It opened and Emma immediately walked into the room, wondering what she would find.

Lord Bargrave was sitting in a chair with Lady Sarah Ann perched on his knee. Emma's breath caught in her chest, and she could do nothing but stare at the sight.

"Whatever is going on here?"

Lady Juliet's sharp tone broke through the astonishment which had wrapped itself around Emma.

"Uncle?"

"What are you doing here? You have not been invited. Remove yourself from my house at once!"

Lady Sarah Ann did not move from where she sat. Her arms gesticulated wildly, but much to Emma's confusion, Lord Bargrave did not move nor speak. In fact, as she took a few steps closer, she saw that his eyes were half-closed and his head lolling forward. Something was dreadfully wrong.

"You must remove yourself from this house at once!" Lady Sarah Ann did not shout, but her voice was a low, angry hiss. "My father will be greatly displeased when he arrives."

In an instant, Emma realized what was planned for Lord Bargrave. Lord Fullerton would arrive to find his daughter perched on Lord Bargrave's knee, alone in the room together. Nothing but matrimony would remove the scandal or the shame, and Lord Bargrave would be obliged to betroth himself to the lady at once.

"Remove yourself from Lord Bargrave."

Hurrying forward, Emma made to reach for Lady Sarah Ann's arm, but the lady flung out one hand towards her, swiping violently.

"I shall do no such thing. *You* are the ones who should —"

"If you do not do so, then you shall be *forcibly* removed." Lady Juliet took a step closer and put both hands on her hips. "At once, Lady Sarah Ann."

"We are aware that you are not used to doing as you are asked but, have no doubt that, in this situation, you will be forced to do as we ask whether you wish to or not."

Emma lifted one eyebrow and waited as Lady Sarah Ann looked from Lady Juliet to her and then back again. Their previous interaction at the ball had evidently left something of an impression, for after a few moments, Lady

Sarah Ann began to get up. Emma and Lady Juliet flew to Lord Bargrave at the very next moment.

"Something is wrong with him."

Emma pressed one hand to his cheek, finding it a little cool. Lord Bargrave's eyes were half-closed, and he did not seem to be able to open them fully, although a low murmur came from the edge of his mouth.

"We must take him home at once." Lady Juliet looked towards Emma and Emma nodded. Even if they had to carry Lord Bargrave from the house, she was determined to do so.

"You cannot. He is needed here!"

Emma ignored Lady Sarah Ann's exclamation, turning to pour a glass of water from the tray in the corner of the room. Bringing it back to Lord Bargrave, she encouraged him to drink and was relieved when he was able to do so. After a moment he drank deeply and then rested his head back against the chair, a sigh breaking from his mouth although his eyes remained closed.

"I believe he may be a little better," Emma murmured, setting the glass aside.

The door suddenly flew open, and Lady Fullerton marched directly into the room, followed by her husband.

"Lord Bargrave, how dare you –"

Her exclamation was cut short as she took in the scene before her. The shining triumph in her eyes quickly faded as both hands went to her hips, her jaw jutting forward as a scowl pulled at her expression.

"Good evening. I did not realize that my daughter had some visitors. Are you all to go to the ball together?" Lord Fullerton's jovial voice broke through the blazing tension which had built in the room. He came forward, the smile falling from his face as he looked at Lord Bargrave. "Lady Juliet, is your uncle unwell?"

Emma shot a quick glance towards Lady Sarah Ann, seeing her opening her mouth, ready to say something which she was sure would attempt to incriminate Lord Bargrave in some way. Thankfully, Lady Juliet had evidently seen the same, for she spoke quickly and with great warmth in her voice.

"How good of you to notice, Lord Fullerton." Lady Juliet patted Lord Bargrave's shoulder. "We were come to hear your daughter's apology to Miss Lawder for striking her without cause. My uncle, however, appears to have taken a little unwell. Might you ask a footman or two to help him to the carriage? It is waiting outside."

"Allow me to seek help directly. Excuse me for a moment."

Stepping outside the room, he left the ladies together and Emma could immediately sense the anger which came from Lady Fullerton and her stepdaughter.

"How dare you?"

Lady Fullerton's harsh words shot to Emma's ears, but she lifted her chin, not intimidated in the least.

"What have you done to my uncle?" Lady Juliet stepped closer to Lady Sarah Ann, her hands clenching to her sides, her face beginning to burn. "Tell me what you have done to him. Tell me at once."

Lady Sarah Ann laughed sharply, putting out one hand and pushing Lady Juliet back.

"It is only a little laudanum."

"Sarah Ann!" Lady Fullerton strode forward, grasping her stepdaughter's arm and pulling her sharply so that she was forced to step back from Lady Juliet. "You are mistaken. Lady Juliet. We have done nothing to your uncle."

"That is not true." Speaking clearly and with great distinction, Emma lifted her gaze to fix it on Lady Fullerton with a determined look. "You were overheard. You had every intention of ensnaring Lord Bargrave, planning to force him into wedlock with Lady Sarah Ann. I do not know your reasons for doing so, but I am certain that was your plan."

Lady Fullerton's lip curled.

"Do you truly think you can garner a confession from me? I will admit to nothing."

"Then expect us to call again very soon, along with my uncle." Lady Juliet lifted an eyebrow. "I am quite certain he will expect your husband to be present also. Perhaps then he will be able to inform him of the reason behind the illness which has taken hold of him at present."

Grim satisfaction spread through Emma's chest as Lady Fullerton paled. She shook her head mutely, but Lady Sarah Ann broke in before anyone else could speak.

"She wished me to marry Lord Bargrave. For whatever reason, she was most insistent... and the truth of the matter is that I found Lord Bargrave more than suitable in every way. When my stepmother determined that *he* was the one I should consider, then I had no reason to disagree."

"And when he rejected your company, you chose, instead, to seek his attentions by another means." Lady Juliet flung out one hand towards her uncle, who was now pinching the bridge of his nose, his head leaning forward. "Why? Why be so insistent on choosing Lord Bargrave?"

"Because I hated him!" With a hiss of breath, Lady Fullerton threw her arms wide. "Do you not understand? My father had long stated that I would marry his widowed acquaintance, Lord Fullerton. I begged for a reprieve and found my attention pulled to Lord Bargrave. I sought to be his for so long – I showed him that I could be everything he needed, knowing that a single *word* from Lord Bargrave could end my father's determined plans. But when the time came for Lord Bargrave to prove himself to me, he did the very opposite. I tried to force his hand, but he rebuffed me even then. He left me to my fate."

Emma could not say a word. The fury in Lady Fullerton's eyes was enough to tell her of the great distress and anger which filled every part of the lady. This had not been for the good of Lord Bargrave, nor for her stepdaughter. In fact, it was solely done as a vendetta, as revenge against the gentleman she believed had injured her, all those years ago.

"My uncle owed you nothing. He owed you no loyalty, despite your demands for it." Lady Juliet narrowed her gaze, her eyes bright with anger. "You tried to manipulate him back then, but you failed. And so you thought to do it again." Lady Fullerton spat out an exclamation but turned her head away, her arms folding across her chest. Lady Juliet turned to Emma. "Had it not been for you, Emma, then I might never have discovered the truth." Taking in a shaking breath, Lady Juliet walked across the room to join Emma, her head held high, but her face quite pale. "It would have been too late for my uncle. You have saved him from a terrible fate."

Before anything further could be said, the door opened and Lord Fullerton, accompanied by two footmen, walked directly into the room.

"I have sent for a physician. He will be at Lord Bargrave's residence within the hour. These two footmen will help your uncle to the carriage. Pray do not be too concerned, Lady Juliet. The physician will know what to do."

Lord Fullerton's smile crashed against the swirling anger which wound its way through the room, grating hard. Emma squeezed Lady Juliet's hand quickly and saw the lady force a smile to her lips.

"Thank you, Lord Fullerton. You are most kind."

Lady Juliet walked directly to the door as the two footmen helped Lord Bargrave to his feet, one of his arms over each of their shoulders. Waiting for them to leave the room, Emma allowed her gaze to linger first on Lady Fullerton, and then on Lady Sarah Ann. Lady Fullerton was nothing but fury. Her face was scarlet, her hands now held tight against her hips and her lips pressed so firmly together, they were white. There was nothing she could do to stop Lord Bargrave from taking his leave of the house. Her plan had failed entirely.

Lady Sarah Ann, on the other hand, seemed quite forlorn. Her shoulders were slumped, and she did not seem to know where to look. Her hands were clasped loosely in front of her, her eyes darting from here to there as she chewed on her bottom lip. It seemed that she now realized, for the first time, that she was not about to get what she wanted.

There was nothing left for Emma to say. Once Lord Bargrave had been helped out to the carriage – and she was quite certain that nothing further could happen to him - she walked from the room with her head held high. Lord Bargrave was safe.

∼

"Your uncle needs only to rest." The physician smiled and patted Lady Juliet's hand. "He will sleep for the rest of the night and be quite back to himself tomorrow. I shall not ask why he took so much laudanum, but I would advise him not to do such a thing again!"

Lady Juliet smiled but said nothing, and Emma noticed the slight tremble around her mouth.

"Thank you for your reassurance. I know it is a great comfort to Lady Juliet." Gesturing to the door, Emma followed the physician as he left the drawing-room. "You have greatly settled her mind and I thank you again on her behalf."

The physician smiled, his clear blue eyes twinkling gently.

"But of course. Encourage Lady Juliet to think of something other than her uncle – it will do her no good to worry for the remainder of the night."

As the physician took his leave, Emma stood quietly by the door for a few minutes, thinking on his final words. *What can we do for the rest of the evening that will take Lady Juliet's mind from her uncle?*

Opening the door, she walked into the room and smiled at Lady Juliet.

"I think that we should go to the ball. We will be late, of course, but that will not matter."

Lady Juliet's eyes flew wide.

"To the ball?" she repeated, as though she was not sure she had heard Emma correctly. "Why should we go there? My uncle is-"

"Your uncle is asleep. He will sleep for the rest of the evening, and until the morning comes. If we linger here, it will only cause you distress and concern. It would be better,

I think., if we made our way to the ball and enjoyed the evening. I believe your uncle would wish us to do so."

"I am not sure... what if Lady Sarah Ann and Lady Fullerton are present?"

Emma smiled softly, her heart filling with determination.

"Then by our very presence, we shall show them that we have not been affected by their actions, and that our resolve and our determination remain. We shall not be turned away from society by their selfish behavior, hiding away in fear of what they might do next. Rather, it is they who should be careful about their presence in London. We know exactly what they have done, even if Lord Fullerton himself does not. That will keep them silent and far from our company. You need not have any fear."

Lady Juliet took a deep breath, set her shoulders, and smiled.

"Very well. When you put it in such a way, I find that I have no cause to refuse. I only hope that my uncle will not waken whilst we are out."

"With the amount of laudanum which he was given, I highly doubt that." Giving her friend a wry smile, Emma turned and made her way to the door. It was not only for Lady Juliet's sake that she insisted on attending the ball but also for her own. It would take her mind from Lord Bargrave and all that he had endured that evening. She could hardly wait to see him come the morrow when, she hoped, he would be in full health once more and be able to tell them both everything that had taken place at Lord Fullerton's home.

CHAPTER FIFTEEN

It was as though a thousand needles were poking themselves into his scalp. Letting out a groan of pain, Giles turned over onto his front to block out the light which tried to push open his eyes.

"You are awake, my Lord." The valet's voice seemed to come from very far away, and Giles could only grimace as his face pressed into the pillow. "Your niece will be most relieved. She has been very concerned about you."

His mind felt cloudy and dull. Taking a deep breath, Giles forced his eyes open and then immediately regretted his action. The light seemed to send screaming pain right into the very depths of his skull and he quickly squeezed his eyes closed again. Whyever should his niece be concerned for him? And why did he feel so very poorly?

"My Lord, the physician advised that you eat something once you awoke. I do not mean to insist, but mayhap it would be a wise idea."

The physician? Struggling to make sense of what his valet said, Giles took another breath and then forced his eyes open again. It seemed to take every ounce of strength he had to push himself up into a sitting position. Whatever was the matter with him?

"Let me help you, my Lord."

"I am quite all right." His voice rasped and his throat ached. "I do feel rather fatigued, however."

"Allow me to bring you breakfast."

Giles nodded, still struggling to look directly at his valet, given the pain in his head. All he wanted to do was lie back down and draw the covers over himself. But instead he pushed himself up against the headboard and waited for the valet to bring his breakfast tray.

"You say that the physician stated that I should eat something?"

The valet nodded.

"Yes, my Lord. He said even a little would help you regain your strength."

Giles blinked rapidly, struggling to recall anything which had occurred the previous evening. He did not remember seeing a physician. He did not remember becoming ill. Whatever had happened?

"Might I be given leave to inform Lady Juliet and Miss Lawder that you are well, my Lord? They have been waiting all morning."

"Of course."

Giles waved a hand and the valet removed himself from the room at once. Picking up his toast, Giles took a bite, and then lifted his cup of coffee to his lips. Whilst he did not feel immediately better, it was as though some strength was returning to him, for his eyes no longer narrowed themselves against the light, and he found himself relaxing against the headboard, his muscles less tight and strained.

What happened last evening?

Frowning hard, Giles chewed on another piece of toast

as he considered. What was the last thing he could remember?

"I received a letter." Muttering to himself, Giles sought to recall who had sent him the note. "There was an urgency to it. I do not..."

In an instant, it all came back to him in a rush. He remembered the letter. He recalled walking into Lady Fullerton's drawing room and being offered a glass of brandy. And then he recalled the weariness which had tied itself to him and refused to release him. He could not recall what had happened after that.

I must see Juliet and Miss Lawder.

Fear sent his heart beating wildly in his chest. His breakfast forgotten, he pushed himself out of bed, staggering slightly due to the weakness in his legs. As he pulled the bell, bringing his valet rushing back into the room, he suddenly realized that he was wearing the same clothes he had been in last evening. His heart beat faster still as he fought against a great and tremendous fear. Just what had Lady Fullerton done to him?

∼

"Juliet. Miss Lawder."

The moment that Giles walked into the drawing room, Miss Lawder and his niece were on their feet, coming towards him with outstretched hands. Miss Lawder seemed to catch herself, and then dropped her hands, choosing to remain where she was and allowing Lady Juliet to embrace him.

"I am so very glad to see you." When Lady Juliet pulled back, her eyes were filled with sparkling tears. "You cannot know of my relief, uncle."

"Nor mine."

Miss Lawder smiled at him, and Giles returned it with one of his own.

"I would beg of you to let me know what the circumstances are at present - and to do so with great urgency. I find myself greatly confused over what took place last evening."

Still feeling a weariness in his limbs, Giles made his way to a chair and sat down a little heavily. Lady Juliet and Miss Lawder followed thereafter, with Miss Lawder pulling the bell before she did so.

"There is nothing for you to fear, Lord Bargrave," she began as Lady Juliet nodded fervently. "I overheard a conversation yesterday afternoon between Lady Sarah Ann and an acquaintance of hers. She spoke of writing an apology but stated that there was a secondary purpose to such a note. At the first, I thought such a letter would come to me. But I was wrong."

Giles ran one hand over his eyes, frowning hard.

"I recall receiving a letter. It was from Lady Sarah Ann, but I do not recall why I went to the house, however."

Lady Juliet and Miss Lawder exchanged a glance.

"You will forgive me, Uncle. I could not help but go in search of this letter. It sat on your desk just as you had left it."

Feeling no anger or frustration that she had done such a thing, Giles leaned forward in his chair, fixing his gaze on his niece.

"And what was said? What made me leave this house and go directly to Lord Fullerton's?"

Lady Juliet pressed her lips tightly together.

"Lady Sarah Ann stated that unless you came directly to tell her that her apology was accepted, Lord Fullerton intended to leave London the very same night. She made it sound as though he had not realized what she had done until that very evening - and you being a gentleman with a very good heart, chose to believe her."

Letting out a heavy sigh, Giles shook his head.

"Perhaps I was a little gullible."

"I do not think so." Miss Lawder spoke up, her eyes filled with a warmth which spread to the very bottom of Giles' toes. "It is as your niece has said: you are a kind-hearted gentleman. Despite all that Lady Fullerton and Lady Sarah Ann had tried to do, you did not want them to leave London unnecessarily."

Something came back to him, and Giles' eyes flared.

"I recall thinking that you had already promised that the matter was forgotten. I did not want to trouble you with it and thus made my way to Lord Fullerton's home with the expectation that I would meet you both at the ball thereafter."

"But that was not their intention. Their intention was to ensnare you, Uncle." Lady Juliet closed her eyes for a moment. "If we had not arrived when we did, then I dread to think what would have occurred."

Giles licked his lips, his stomach twisting. Part of him did not wish to hear of the situation they had found him in, but yet he knew that he needed to hear the truth.

"What happened?"

"It was Miss Lawder's doing. She insisted that we make our way to Lady Fullerton's home at once. Once I understood her reasons for doing so, I agreed wholeheartedly. Our fear was very great, increased all the more when the butler would not permit us entry to the house."

A rueful smile crept across Giles' face.

"Knowing you both as I do, I presume that did not cause

any particular difficulty."

Miss Lawder winced.

"You do know us well, my Lord. In a most improper manner, we forced our way into the house and began to search the rooms. I could not do anything else, believing, as I did, that Lady Sarah Ann and Lady Fullerton had naught but nefarious intentions for you."

"I am very grateful that you behaved as you did." Blowing out a long breath, Giles closed his eyes and braced himself for what was to come. "And what did you see when you found me? I recall being offered a glass of brandy and thereafter feeling very tired, but after that, I can recall nothing else."

There came a short pause.

"When we arrived, Lady Sarah Ann was perched on your knee. There was no one else in the room."

Giles's eyes flew open, and he stared at Miss Lawder, but she nodded slowly, as if to confirm all that he had just heard from her.

"She refused to move. It was only after some persuasion that she finally stood up." Lady Juliet's cheeks were a little red. "We could see what their intention was. Shortly thereafter, Lady Fullerton arrived with Lord Fullerton behind her, clearly expecting the room to be quite empty, save for you and her stepdaughter."

"They wished to force me into matrimony. Just as Lady Fullerton herself had attempted to do, some years ago." The horror of what he could have fallen into, had it not been for Miss Lawder's sharp mind, spread out in front of him, like a deep and dark valley. "Why? I do not understand."

A cold hand grasped at his heart, and he shivered violently, his gaze turning to Miss Lawder and then to Lady Juliet.

"I believe that Lady Fullerton does not... think well of you."

The hesitant way that Miss Lawder spoke told Giles a good deal more.

"You mean to say that she despises me. This was to be her punishment, was it? Her punishment for my refusing to wed her some years ago."

"That is it, precisely, uncle." Lady Juliet shook her head. "Knowing just how awful Lady Sarah Ann is, I believe that Lady Fullerton thought it a just punishment for you to endure such a wife for the remainder of your days."

"And mayhap she is also aware that it will be difficult for her stepdaughter to find a husband, given her character." Miss Lawder shrugged. "I do not mean to justify what she did, merely to explain it."

Blowing out a long breath, Giles dropped his head into his hands, his fingers pushing through into his hair.

"I confess that I am greatly disturbed by what has taken place."

"But you have been saved from it. That must be a relief, surely?"

Giles nodded but kept his eyes closed. It was a very great relief to know that he had been spared from the dark plans of Lady Fullerton – but what concerned him now was that she might attempt to do the very same thing to another gentleman. It would not be driven by hate, as it had been with him, but rather more the fear that her stepdaughter would never find a husband otherwise.

"I cannot find words to express to you both the depths of my gratitude." Opening his eyes, he looked first at his niece and then at Miss Lawder. "If you had not been concerned enough to do as you did, then I would now find myself betrothed to Lady Sarah Ann."

"You may place your gratitude solely on the shoulders of Miss Lawder, uncle." Lady Juliet rose from her chair and walked over to her companion, setting one hand on her shoulder as she looked toward him. "I would not have known of any of this had it not been for her. We would not have made our way to Lord Fullerton's home. We would not have pushed our way into his house and found you in such a situation, had it not been for Miss Lawder's determination. It is to her that you owe your gratitude, Uncle. All of it."

Miss Lawder's face burned red, and she shook her head.

"That is nonsense. You were just as concerned as I and just as –"

"No, I shall not have you refute me." Lady Juliet laughed and squeezed her companion's shoulder before returning to her seat. "You are the most wonderful lady, Miss Lawder. We are both grateful to have you with us, I am sure - now more than ever."

"With that, I must wholeheartedly agree." Were it appropriate, Giles would rise from his chair and embrace Miss Lawder so that he might offer a small gesture of his relief and gratitude towards her. "However, I shall not let the matter lie."

His niece's eyes widened.

"What do you intend to do?"

Giles got to his feet.

"I intend to speak to Lord Fullerton, to Lady Fullerton, and to Lady Sarah Ann."

"But why should you do such a thing?" Miss Lawder blinked, then shook her head. "I do not mean to question you, but you must be aware that you will cause a great upset."

"I have no intention of spreading any gossip through the *ton*. However, have either of you considered the fact that

Lady Fullerton and Lady Sarah Ann might do such a thing again? They may set their eyes on another gentleman entirely, and do the very same to him - and perhaps, this time, succeed. After all, we are all aware that Lady Sarah Ann will struggle to make a suitable match, given her character. Her father and her stepmother will want her to marry above her station, if possible, but given that the *ton* is slowly becoming aware of her foibles, she may find it very difficult indeed to do such a thing. No gentleman will want a wife with a short temper and a demanding nature, no matter how much her dowry may be."

Miss Lawder nodded slowly.

"Your concern for your fellow gentlemen is admirable."

His niece nodded.

"When will you go?"

"At this very moment." Slapping both hands to his knees, Giles pushed himself up to standing, ignoring the lingering weakness in his limbs. "I have a much better chance of seeing them all at home if I go early."

"I do hope that it goes as well as it can." Miss Lawder rose to her feet and came towards him. "I am very glad to see you so well, my Lord."

The urge to step forward and take her into his arms was so strong that Giles almost did that very thing, even in front of his niece. He held her gaze steadily for some moments in complete silence, wishing that he could express to her all that was in his heart at present.

Now is not the moment for it. But upon my return, I shall tell her all.

"My visit will not be of a long duration. I expect I shall return within the hour." Giving them both a short sharp bow, he turned on his heel and marched from the room. He would tell Lord Fullerton everything, in the hope that he would spare some poor unfortunate gentleman from the very same fate that Giles had only just escaped - and the consequences thereafter would be entirely for Lord Fullerton to lay out.

∼

"Good morning."

Stepping into the breakfast room, Giles gave a quick bow, then lifted his head. Lady Fullerton had frozen in place, her hand poised over her plate. Lady Sarah Ann's eyes had gone very wide indeed, and Lord Fullerton was the only one smiling.

"Good morning to you, Lord Bargrave. You find us breaking our fast."

"And I apologize for calling upon you so early. The matter, I am afraid, would not wait."

The clatter of a fork falling onto a plate had everyone's eyes turning to Lady Fullerton. Blinking rapidly, she shook her head and made to stand.

"You will not require myself and my stepdaughter to be present. We shall excuse ourselves, of course."

"Wait a moment." Gesturing with one hand, Giles motioned for her to remain in her seat. "As I am sure you are aware, Lady Fullerton, this matter concerns both you, your stepdaughter, and myself."

Lord Fullerton harrumphed, picking up his napkin and dabbing at his mouth.

"It concerns my wife and daughter?" He repeated, a thick line forming between his eyebrows. "Whatever do you mean, Lord Bargrave?"

Giles cleared his throat, put his hands behind his back and lifted one eyebrow in the direction of Lady Fullerton.

She had gone very pale indeed, but turned her head away, looking stubbornly down at her plate so that she would not have to even glance at him.

"I come to inform you of this Lord Fullerton, out of concern for other gentlemen of the *ton*. You have my word that I shall not spread rumor nor speak a single word of gossip in amongst society."

Lord Fullerton's eyes rounded, fixing themselves to Giles.

"This sounds rather grave."

"That is because it is of the utmost seriousness. Lord Fullerton, I am come to tell you that your wife and your stepdaughter attempted to put me in a situation that I would be entirely unable to extricate myself from."

Lord Fullerton blinked, then turned his gaze towards his wife. She did not move, and it appeared that her lack of response gave Lord Fullerton the confirmation he needed that what Giles was saying was the truth.

"I do not understand." Turning back to look at Giles, Lord Fullerton's tone remained calm. "What situation are you speaking of?"

"I am speaking of what took place last evening."

"When you became unwell?"

"I was not unwell, Lord Fullerton. Your daughter had poured me a brandy. The glass, it turned out, did not only contain brandy, but also laudanum. I will admit to finding the taste a little strange at the time, but thought it rude to leave it aside, so thus, I drank it all. I awoke this morning with no recollection of what had taken place the previous night. However, to my eternal gratitude, my niece and her companion came in search of me. Miss Lawder had previously overheard concerning conversations on two separate occasions – one between Lady Fullerton and Lady Sarah

Ann, and the second between Lady Sarah Ann and a friend. It soon became clear to her that your wife and your daughter were planning, together, to force me into matrimony."

Lord Fullerton's eyes widened all the more, and he turned his head slowly in the direction of his wife.

Silence fell across the room. Giles held his breath, for if Lady Fullerton denied all and Lady Sarah Ann did the same, then Lord Fullerton himself might refuse to believe the story to be true.

"My dear." Lord Fullerton's expression was still calm, but his voice held a heavy note. "You need to give some response to what Lord Bargrave has laid at your door."

Lady Fullerton and Lady Sarah Ann exchanged a glance.

"It is not my fault!" The moment that those words fell from Lady Sarah Ann's lips, Giles let out such a long breath of relief that even Lord Fullerton looked in his direction. He did not need to worry any longer - the truth was out. "I only did as my stepmother told me. She said that I would struggle to find a husband - which I could not quite believe - but she was most insistent." Lady Sarah Ann shrugged, turning her head slightly away. "But I could not complain when it came to Lord Bargrave. His attributes were made quite clear to me, and I considered that I should be rather fortunate to become his wife."

"You have said quite enough, Sarah Ann." Lady Fullerton spoke sharply, slicing the air between herself and her stepdaughter with her hand. "Your father does not need to know any further details."

"I believe that *I* shall be the judge of that!" Lord Fullerton rose from his chair, planting both hands on the table. "I cannot quite believe that you have done this. I am utterly horrified." His voice grew slowly louder, but Lady Fullerton was on her feet in a moment.

"I have been doing my very best for your daughter, can you not see that? It is not as though she has caught the eye of any gentleman! There are whispers and gossip about her temper already flooding through the *ton* - And I cannot refute any of them, for they are all true! How am I meant to find her a match when she behaves thus?"

"And so, you thought to trick Lord Bargrave into matrimony? I do not wish to know the particulars of what went on, but I can only imagine that I was meant to stumble upon a particular scene, is that not so?"

"It is all that Lord Bargrave deserves! He..." Lady Fullerton's red cheeks suddenly faded to white as she realized what she had been about to say. Wide eyes made their way from Lord Fullerton towards Giles, but he chose not to respond.

"I cannot imagine that Lord Bargrave has ever behaved so poorly that it merits any sort of punishment, particularly from you!" Lord Fullerton shook his head, then glared at his wife. "Regardless of your opinion about my daughter, there is no need for any such behavior. It is cruel. It is *unspeakably* cruel. I am heartily ashamed of you both."

Giles cleared his throat, having no wish to remain for any further discussions.

"As I have said, Lord Fullerton, I have come only to inform you of what took place, so that nothing like this may occur to any other gentleman in London."

Lord Fullerton swung a furious gaze towards him. "I do not know what to say. Lord Bargrave. I am horrified. I am astounded. I can hardly take in what has been revealed to me this morning. My wife and my daughter, it seems, are not known to me! I promise, you must know, that I never once gave my consent to such actions. I would never do such a thing."

"And I believe you. I have no wish to spread this news to anyone else in society and you have my word that Lady Juliet and Miss Lawder will not do so either. Nor do I demand any particular consequences. I consider this matter to be solely in your hands, Lord Fullerton."

The gentleman closed his eyes, his hands still pressed flat on the table, his shoulders rounding.

"That is a good deal more grace than my wife and my daughter deserve."

For a moment, the figure of Miss Lawder came into his mind, causing Giles to smile.

"I have been shown a good deal of grace myself. It is because of that fact that I share such a thing with your family also. I will depart now, so long as I have your assurance that this... this *trickery* will never take place again."

Lord Fullerton passed one hand over his eyes, then held it out towards Giles.

"You have my solemn word."

"I thank you."

Shaking the man's hand briefly, Giles gave the gentleman a nod and then turned away without another word. He did not glance towards Lady Fullerton or Lady Sarah Ann, fully aware that he was leaving a great deal of difficulty behind him, but relieved, nonetheless, that he had chosen to do so. The thoughts of Miss Lawder remained in his mind as he left the house. Suddenly all he wanted to do was make his way home and be in her presence again. There was so much he had to say, so much that he wanted to declare to her, and once he returned, Giles had no intention of hesitating for a single moment. By the end of the day, Miss Lawder would know the truth of his heart.

CHAPTER SIXTEEN

"Do you think that the matter has been resolved?"

"I do not think that such a thing can be resolved. I think that Lord Bargrave will tell Lord Fullerton the truth, and that will be the end of it."

Unable to seat herself due to swirling tension in her limbs, Emma began to pace up and down the drawing-room, clasping her hands together tightly.

"I only hope that Lord Fullerton will accept it without question. There is a chance that he may doubt Lord Bargrave's words and claim loyalty to his wife and daughter."

Lady Juliet shook her head.

"I think that I – oh!"

Hearing the sound of a carriage approaching both she and Emma rushed to the window.

"It is my uncle," Lady Juliet breathed, seeing the carriage pulled to a stop just outside the house. Relief flooded Emma's soul and she closed her eyes, releasing a breath she had not known she had been holding. "Look, he is waving at us."

Emma opened her eyes just in time to see Lord Bargrave grin before he turned and marched into the house.

"From his expression, I must believe that all has gone well."

Lady Juliet turned towards the door, and they waited expectantly. After only a few moments, it was opened and Lord Bargrave walked in, his face wreathed in smiles.

"You smile, Uncle. I assume that all has gone well?"

Lord Bargrave shook his head.

"You do not find me smiling because it was a pleasant experience, but rather because of the gladness that fills my heart at being home with you both." He made to come a little closer, then stopped. His smile faded, his eyes turning from Lady Juliet towards Emma and then back again. "And to think that I was unwilling to have you both reside with me this summer. What would I have done without you?"

"As I have said, Uncle, it has been Miss Lawder's doing more than my own." Lady Juliet glanced towards Emma, smiled, and then tilted her head towards the door. "If you will excuse me for a few moments, I must go and speak to the housekeeper. I believe our dinner this evening should be a celebratory one."

Emma's breath caught in her chest, and she shook her head wordlessly, but Lady Juliet ignored her entirely. Within a few minutes, Emma found herself quite alone with Lord Bargrave – and he had such a look in his eyes that heat began immediately to build in her cheeks.

"Miss Lawder – Emma." The way he spoke her name seemed to send sunshine streaming through the windows, the heat of its rays burning her skin. Sparks spun in her vision, but she could look nowhere but his face. "The day you walked through my door was the very best day of my life - even though, at the time, I did not know it." He came a little closer to her and her heart began to beat with such a frantic rhythm that she clasped her hands in front of her chest to drown out the sound. "You have saved me from so many things. Yes, you saved me from Lady Sarah Ann and from Lady Fullerton's clutches - but your determination and your strength have shown me that I needed to be saved from myself."

Swallowing hard, Emma stared up into his eyes, fumbling for what she ought to say. Lord Bargrave came so close to her that she could feel his breath brush across her cheek and, much to her embarrassment, the sensation elicited a gasp from her lips.

"Ah..."

Lord Bargrave only smiled.

"I look back on my life, look back upon these previous Seasons and I realize that I was lost in a cloud of selfishness. The idea of matrimony, of being committed to one other living soul for the remaining days of my life seemed almost laughable, whereas now I can think of nothing more honorable." Gentle fingers brushed lightly across her cheek before resting on her shoulder and skimming down her arm to catch her hand with his. "I can think of nothing I want more."

Her chest tightened as she slowly realized that he was speaking of marriage... with her. Her eyes flared and she found herself gripping his hand with such a fierceness that Lord Bargrave jerked in surprise, then chuckled.

"Yes, my dear Emma. I am asking you if you would consider marrying me. I know that I have failed you many times – in my behavior towards you when you first arrived and, thereafter, when Lady Sarah Ann struck you because of what I had said – but I must pray that you are willing to forgive my mistakes and foolishness." Coming even closer, he began to lower his head, his voice husky with emotion. "I must hope that you are feeling *something* akin to what is in my heart."

Emma swallowed against the ache in her throat, her heart swelling with so much happiness that it felt as if it would explode from within her chest at any moment.

"And might I ask what is in your heart, Lord Bargrave?"

Lord Bargrave threw back his head and laughed, shaking his head at her.

"Even now, you display the very same boldness that I have come to admire and respect." His smile faded into tenderness as his free hand lifted to her face, his thumb running across her cheek, his sea-blue eyes searching her own. "Love is in my heart, Emma. Love for you. It has grown steadily and, at times, I have fought not only to deny it but also to ignore it – but yet it has refused to remain unseen. Interest blossomed into affection and affection grew to love." Taking a breath, he smiled softly. "I love you, Emma. I want you very much to be my wife."

It was as though all the birds began to sing their beautiful songs in one moment, for the sheer joy that poured into Emma's heart was enough to catapult her into exultation. She had never allowed herself to hope for this, had never once even let herself *think* of what could be – and now here it was, being offered to her without hesitation.

"I love you too, Lord Bargrave." Her smile suddenly faded. "But what of Lady Juliet?"

Lord Bargrave frowned.

"What do you mean?"

"I – I am her companion, I am meant to be –"

"And you can *still* be so, if you wish it. You will be everything you are to her at present, but without the title of companion." Lord Bargrave leaned down and brushed his lips against her forehead, making her eyes flutter closed as her senses whirled. "Instead, I think a better title would be that of 'Aunt'."

Her eyes flew open as she stared up at him, only realizing now that, in marrying Lord Bargrave, she would forever be tied to Lady Juliet. A beautiful smile spread across her face as Lord Bargrave chuckled, his thumb gently lifting her chin.

"Then what say you, my dear Emma? Will you marry me?"

Emma flung her arms around his neck, letting him hold her tight as she sighed with both happiness and contentment. Everything had fallen into place, giving her more than she had ever dreamed for.

"Yes, my dearest Bargrave. Yes, I shall be your bride."

One more companion finds happiness! I am happy for her... and happy for Lord Bargrave who narrowly missed a lifetime sentence married to an unsuitable lady, thanks to Emma!

Please check out the first book in the series if you missed it! More Than a Companion See a sneak peak just ahead!

MY DEAR READER

Thank you for reading and supporting my books! I hope this story brought you some escape from the real world into the always captivating Regency world. A good story, especially one with a happy ending, just brightens your day and makes you feel good! If you enjoyed the book, would you leave a review on Amazon? Reviews are always appreciated.

Below is a complete list of all my books! Why not click and see if one of them can keep you entertained for a few hours?

The Duke's Daughters Series
The Duke's Daughters: A Sweet Regency Romance Boxset
A Rogue for a Lady
My Restless Earl
Rescued by an Earl
In the Arms of an Earl
The Reluctant Marquess (Prequel)

A Smithfield Market Regency Romance
The Smithfield Market Romances: A Sweet Regency Romance Boxset
The Rogue's Flower
Saved by the Scoundrel
Mending the Duke
The Baron's Malady

The Returned Lords of Grosvenor Square
The Returned Lords of Grosvenor Square: A Regency Romance Boxset
The Waiting Bride
The Long Return
The Duke's Saving Grace
A New Home for the Duke

The Spinsters Guild
The Spinsters Guild: A Sweet Regency Romance Boxset
A New Beginning
The Disgraced Bride
A Gentleman's Revenge
A Foolish Wager
A Lord Undone

Convenient Arrangements
Convenient Arrangements: A Regency Romance Collection
A Broken Betrothal
In Search of Love
Wed in Disgrace
Betrayal and Lies
A Past to Forget
Engaged to a Friend

Landon House
Mistaken for a Rake
A Selfish Heart
A Love Unbroken
A Christmas Match
A Most Suitable Bride
An Expectation of Love

Second Chance Regency Romance
Loving the Scarred Soldier
Second Chance for Love
A Family of her Own
A Spinster No More

Soldiers and Sweethearts
To Trust a Viscount
Whispers of the Heart
Dare to Love a Marquess
Healing the Earl
A Lady's Brave Heart

Ladies on their Own: Governesses and Companions
More Than a Companion
The Hidden Governess
The Companion and the Earl
More than a Governess
Protected by the Companion

Christmas Stories
Love and Christmas Wishes: Three Regency Romance Novellas
A Family for Christmas
Mistletoe Magic: A Regency Romance
Heart, Homes & Holidays: A Sweet Romance Anthology

Happy Reading!

All my love,

Rose

A SNEAK PEEK OF MORE THAN A COMPANION

PROLOGUE

"Did you hear me, Honora?"

Miss Honora Gregory lifted her head at once, knowing that her father did not refer to her as 'Honora' very often and that he only did so when he was either irritated or angry with her.

"I do apologize, father, I was lost in my book," Honora replied, choosing to be truthful with her father rather than make excuses, despite the ire she feared would now follow. "Forgive my lack of consideration."

This seemed to soften Lord Greene just a little, for his scowl faded and his lips were no longer taut.

"I shall only repeat myself the once," her father said firmly, although there was no longer that hint of frustration in his voice. "There is very little money, Nora. I cannot give you a Season."

All thought of her book fled from Honora's mind as her eyes fixed to her father's, her chest suddenly tight. She had known that her father was struggling financially, although she had never been permitted to be aware of the details. But not to have a Season was deeply upsetting, and Honora had to immediately fight back hot tears which sprang into her eyes. There had always been a little hope in her heart, had always been a flicker of expectation that, despite knowing her father's situation, he might still be able to take her to London."

"Your aunt, however, is eager to go to London," Lord Greene continued, as Honora pressed one hand to her stomach in an attempt to soothe the sudden rolling and writhing which had captured her. He waved a hand dismissively, his expression twisting. "I do not know the reasons for it, given that she is widowed and, despite that, happily settled, but it seems she is determined to have some time in London this summer. Therefore, whilst you are not to have a Season of your own – you will not be presented or the like – you will go with your aunt to London."

Honora swallowed against the tightness in her throat, her hands twisting at her gown as she fought against a myriad of emotions.

"I am to be her companion?" she said, her voice only just a whisper as her father nodded.

She had always been aware that Lady Langdon, her aunt, had only ever considered her own happiness and her own situation, but to invite your niece to London as your companion rather than chaperone her for a Season surely spoke of selfishness!

"It is not what you might have hoped for, I know," her father continued, sounding resigned as a small sigh escaped his lips, his shoulders slumping. Honora looked up at him, seeing him now a little grey and realizing the full extent of his weariness. Some of her upset faded as she took in her father's demeanor, knowing that his lack of financial security was not his doing. The estate lands had done poorly these last three years, what with drought one year and flooding the next. As such, money had been ploughed into the ground to restore it and yet it would not become profitable again for at least another year. She could not blame her father for that. And yet, her heart had struggled against such news, trying to be glad that she would be in London but broken-hearted to learn that her aunt wanted her as her companion and nothing more. "I will not join you, of course," Lord Greene continued, coming a little closer to Honora and tilting his head just a fraction, studying his daughter carefully and, perhaps, all too aware of her inner turmoil. "You can, of course, choose to refuse your aunt's invitation – but I can offer you nothing more than what is being given to you at present, Nora. This may be your only opportunity to be in London."

Honora blinked rapidly against the sudden flow of hot tears that threatened to pour from her eyes, should she permit them.

"It is very good of my aunt," she managed to say, trying to be both gracious and thankful whilst ignoring the other, more negative feelings which troubled her. "Of course, I shall go."

Lord Greene smiled sadly, then reached out and settled one hand on Honora's shoulder, bending down just a little as he did so.

"My dear girl, would that I could give you more. You already have enough to endure, with the loss of your mother when you were just a child yourself. And now you have a poor father who cannot provide for you as he ought."

"I understand, Father," Honora replied quickly, not wanting to have her father's soul laden with guilt. "Pray, do not concern yourself. I shall be contented enough with what Lady Langdon has offered me."

Her father closed his eyes and let out another long sigh, accompanied this time with a shake of his head.

"She may be willing to allow you a little freedom, my dear girl," he said, without even the faintest trace of hope in his voice. "My sister has always been inclined to think only of herself, but there may yet be a change in her character."

Honora was still trying to accept the news that she was to be a companion to her aunt and could not make even a murmur of agreement. She closed her eyes, seeing a vision of herself standing in a ballroom, surrounded by ladies and gentlemen of the *ton*. She could almost hear the music, could almost feel the warmth on her skin... and then realized that she would be sitting quietly at the back of the room, able only to watch, and not to engage with any of it. Pain etched itself across her heart and Honora let out a long, slow breath, allowing the news to sink into her very soul.

"Thank you, Father." Her voice was hoarse but her words heartfelt, knowing that her father was doing his very best for her in the circumstances. "I will be a good companion for my aunt."

"I am sure that you will be, my dear," he said, quietly. "And I will pray that, despite everything, you might find a match – even in the difficulties that face us."

The smile faded from Honora's lips as, with that, her father left the room. There was very little chance of such a thing happening, as she was to be a companion rather than a debutante. The realization that she would be an afterthought, a lady worth nothing more than a mere glance from the moment that she set foot in London, began to tear away at Honora's heart, making her brow furrow and her lips pull downwards. There could be no moments of sheer enjoyment for her, no time when she was not considering all that was required of her as her aunt's companion. She would have to make certain that her thoughts were always fixed on her responsibilities, that her intentions were settled on her aunt at all times. Yes, there would be gentlemen to smile at and, on the rare chance, mayhap even converse with, but her aunt would not often permit such a thing, she was sure. Lady Langdon had her own reasons for going to London for the Season, whatever they were, and Honora was certain she would take every moment for herself.

"I must be grateful," Honora murmured to herself, setting aside her book completely as she rose from her chair and meandered towards the window.

Looking out at the grounds below, she took in the gardens, the pond to her right and the rose garden to her left. There were so many things here that held such beauty and, with it, such fond memories that there was a part of her, Honora had to admit, which did not want to leave it, did not want to set foot in London where she might find herself in a new and lower situation. There was security here, a comfort which encouraged her to remain, which told her to hold fast to all that she knew – but Honora was all too aware that she could not. Her future was not here. When her father passed away, if she was not wed, then Honora knew that she would be left to continue on as a companion, just to make certain that she had a home and enough coin for her later years. That was not the future she wanted but, she considered, it might very well be all that she could gain. Tears began to swell in her eyes, and she dropped her head, squeezing her eyes closed and forcing the tears back. This was the only opportunity she would have to go to London and, whilst it was not what she had hoped for, Honora had to accept it for what it was and begin to prepare herself for leaving her father's house – possibly, she considered, for good. Clasping both hands together, Honora drew in a long breath and let it out slowly as her eyes closed and her shoulders dropped.

A new part of her life was beginning. A new and unexpected future was being offered to her, and Honora had no other choice but to grasp it with both hands.

CHAPTER ONE

Pushing all doubt aside, Robert walked into White's with the air of someone who expected not only to be noticed, but to be greeted and exclaimed over in the most exaggerated manner. His chin lifted as he snapped his fingers towards one of the waiting footmen, giving him his request for the finest of brandies in short, sharp words. Then, he continued to make his way inside, his hands swinging loosely by his sides, his shoulders pulled back and his chest a little puffed out.

"Goodness, is that you?"

Robert grinned, his expectations seeming to be met, as a gentleman to his left rose to his feet and came towards him, only for him to stop suddenly and shake his head.

"Forgive me, you are not Lord Johnstone," he said, holding up both hands, palms out, towards Robert. "I thought that you were he, for you have a very similar appearance."

Grimacing, Robert shrugged and said not a word, making his way past the gentleman and finding a slight heat rising into his face. To be mistaken for another was one thing, but to remain entirely unrecognized was quite another! His doubts attempted to come rushing back. Surely someone would remember him, would remember what he had done last Season?

"Lord Crampton, good evening."

Much to his relief, Robert heard his title being spoken and turned his head to the right, seeing a gentleman sitting in a high-backed chair, a glass of brandy in his hand and a small smile on his face as he looked up at Robert.

"Good evening, Lord Marchmont," Robert replied, glad indeed that someone, at least, had recognized him. "I am back in London, as you can see."

"I hope you find it a pleasant visit," came the reply, only for Lord Marchmont to turn away and continue speaking to another gentleman sitting opposite – a man whom Robert had neither seen, nor was acquainted with. There was no suggestion from Lord Marchmont about introducing Robert to him and, irritated, Robert turned sharply away. His head dropped, his shoulders rounded, and he did not even attempt to keep his frustration out of his expression. His jaw tightened, his eyes blazed and his hands balled into fists.

Had they all forgotten him so quickly?

Practically flinging himself into a large, overstuffed armchair in the corner of White's, Robert began to mutter darkly to himself, almost angry about how he had been treated. Last Season he had been the talk of London! Why should he be so easily forgotten now? Unpleasant memories rose, of being inconspicuous, and disregarded, when he had first inherited his title. He attempted to push them aside, but his upset grew steadily so that even the brandy he was given by the footman – who had spent some minutes trying to find Lord Crampton — tasted like ash in his mouth. Nothing took his upset away and Robert wrapped it around his shoulders like a blanket, huddling against it and keeping it close to him.

He had not expected this. He had hoped to be not only remembered but celebrated! When he stepped into a room, he thought that he should be noticed. He *wanted* his name to be murmured by others, for it to be spread around the room that he had arrived! Instead, he was left with an almost painful frustration that he had been so quickly forgotten by the *ton* who, only a few months ago, had been his adoring admirers.

"Another brandy might help remove that look from your face." Robert did not so much as blink, hearing the man's voice but barely acknowledging it. "You are upset, I can tell." The man rose and came to sit opposite Robert, who finally was forced to recognize him. "That is no way for a gentleman to appear upon his first few days in London!"

Robert's lip curled. He should not, he knew, express his frustration so openly, but he found that he could not help himself.

"Good evening, Lord Burnley," he muttered, finding the man's broad smile and bright eyes to be nothing more than an irritation. "Are *you* enjoying the London Season thus far?"

Lord Burnley chuckled, his eyes dancing - which added to Robert's irritation all the more. He wanted to turn his head away, to make it plain to Lord Burnley that he did not enjoy his company and wanted very much to be free of it, but his standing as a gentleman would not permit him to do so.

"I have only been here a sennight but yes, I have found

a great deal of enjoyment thus far," Lord Burnley told him. "But you should expect that, should you not? After all, a gentleman coming to London for the Season comes for good company, fine wine, excellent conversation and to be in the company of beautiful young ladies – one of whom might even catch his eye!"

This was, of course, suggestive of the fact that Lord Burnley might have had his head turned already by one of the young women making their come out, but Robert was in no mood to enter such a discussion. Instead, he merely sighed, picked up his glass again and held it out to the nearby footman, who came over to them at once.

"Another," he grunted, as the man took his glass from him. "And for Lord Burnley here."

Lord Burnley chuckled again, the sound grating on Robert's skin.

"I am quite contented with what I have at present, although I thank you for your consideration," he replied, making Robert's brow lift in surprise. What sort of gentleman turned down the opportunity to drink fine brandy? Half wishing that Lord Burnley would take his leave so that he might sit here in silence and roll around in his frustration, Robert settled back in his chair, his arms crossed over his chest and his gaze turned away from Lord Burnley in the vain hope that this would encourage the man to take his leave. He realized that he was behaving churlishly, yet somehow, he could not prevent it – he had hoped so much, and so far, nothing was as he had expected. "So, you are returned to London," Lord Burnley said, making Robert roll his eyes at the ridiculous observation which, for whatever reason, Lord Burnley either did not notice or chose to ignore. "Do you have any particular intentions for this Season?"

Sending a lazy glance towards Lord Burnley, Robert shrugged.

"If you mean to ask whether or not I intend to pursue one particular young lady with the thought of matrimony in mind, then I must tell you that you are mistaken to even *think* that I should care for such a thing," he stated, plainly. "I am here only to enjoy myself."

"I see."

Lord Burnley gave no comment in judgment of Robert's statement, but Robert felt it nonetheless, quite certain that Lord Burnley now thought less of him for being here solely for his own endeavors. He scowled. Lord Burnley might have decided that it was the right time for him to wed, but Robert had no intention of doing so whatsoever. Given his good character, given his standing and his title, there would be very few young ladies who would suit him, and Robert knew that it would take a significant effort not only to first identify such a young lady but also to then make certain that she would suit him completely. It was not something that he wanted to put his energy into at present. For the moment, Robert had every intention of simply dancing and conversing and mayhap even calling upon the young ladies of the *ton,* but that would be for his own enjoyment rather than out of any real consideration.

Besides which, he told himself, *given that the* ton *will, no doubt, remember all that you did last Season, there will be many young ladies seeking out your company which would make it all the more difficult to choose only one, should you have any inclination to do so!*

"And are you to attend Lord Newport's ball tomorrow evening?"

Being pulled from his thoughts was an irritating interruption and Robert let the long sigh fall from his lips without hesitation, sending it in Lord Burnley's direction who, much to Robert's frustration, did not even react to it.

"I am," Robert replied, grimacing. "Although I do hope that the other guests will not make too much of my arrival. I should not like to steal any attention away from Lord and Lady Newport."

Allowing himself a few moments of study, Robert looked back at Lord Burnley and waited to see if there was even a hint of awareness in his expression. Lord Burnley, however, merely shrugged one shoulder and turned his head away, making nothing at all of what Robert had told him. Gritting his teeth, Robert closed his eyes and tried to force out another long, calming breath. He did not need Lord Burnley to remember what he had done, nor to celebrate it. What was important was that the ladies of the *ton* recalled it, for then he would be more than certain to have their attention for the remainder of the Season – and that was precisely what Robert wanted. Their attention would elevate him in the eyes of the *ton*, would bring him into sharp relief against the other gentlemen who were enjoying the Season in London. He did not care what the gentlemen thought of him, he reminded himself, for their considerations were of no importance save for the fact that they might be able to invite him to various social occasions.

Robert's shoulders dropped and he opened his eyes. Coming to White's this evening had been a mistake. He ought to have made his way to some soiree or other, for he had many invitations already but, given that he had only arrived in London the day before, had thought it too early to make his entrance into society. That had been a mistake. The *ton* ought to know of his arrival just as soon as was possible, so that his name might begin to be whispered amongst them. He could not bear the idea that the pleasant notoriety he had experienced last Season might have faded already!

A small smile pulled at his lips as he considered this, his heart settling into a steady rhythm, free from frustration and upset now. Surely, it was not that he was not remembered by society, but rather that he had chosen the wrong place to make his entrance. The gentlemen of London would not make his return to society of any importance, given that they would be jealous and envious of his desirability in the eyes of the ladies of the *ton*, and therefore, he ought not to have expected such a thing from them! A quiet chuckle escaped his lips as Robert shook his head, passing one hand over his eyes for a moment. It had been a simple mistake and that mistake had brought him irritation and confusion – but that would soon be rectified, once he made his way into full London society.

"You appear to be in better spirits now, Lord Crampton."

Robert's brow lifted as he looked back at Lord Burnley, who was studying him with mild interest.

"I have just come to a realization," he answered, not wanting to go into a detailed explanation but at the same time, wanting to answer Lord Burnley's question. "I had hoped that I might have been greeted a little more warmly but, given my history, I realize now that I ought not to have expected it from a group of gentlemen."

Lord Burnley frowned.

"Your history?"

Robert's jaw tightened, wondering if it was truly that Lord Burnley did not know of what he spoke, or if he was saying such a thing simply to be a little irritating.

"You do not know?" he asked, his own brows drawing low over his eyes as he studied Lord Burnley's open expression. The man shook his head, his head tipping gently to one side in a questioning manner. "I am surprised. It was the talk of London!"

"Then I am certain you will be keen to inform me of it," Lord Burnley replied, his tone neither dull nor excited, making Robert's brow furrow all the more. "Was it something of significance?"

Robert gritted his teeth, finding it hard to believe that Lord Burnley, clearly present at last year's Season, did not know of what he spoke. For a moment, he thought he would not inform the fellow about it, given that he did not appear to be truly interested in what they spoke of, but then his pride won out and he began to explain.

"Are you acquainted with Lady Charlotte Fortescue?" he asked, seeing Lord Burnley shake his head. "She is the daughter of the Duke of Strathaven. Last Season, when I had only just stepped into the title of the Earl of Crampton, I discovered her being pulled away through Lord Kingsley's gardens by a most uncouth gentleman and, of course, in coming to her rescue, I struck the fellow a blow that had him knocked unconscious." His chin lifted slightly as he recalled that moment, remembering how Lady Charlotte had practically collapsed into his arms in the moments after he had struck the despicable Viscount Forthside and knocked him to the ground. Her father, the Duke of Strathaven, had been in search of his daughter and had found them both only a few minutes later, quickly followed by the Duchess of Strathaven. In fact, a small group of gentlemen and ladies had appeared in the gardens and had applauded him for his rescue – and news of it had quickly spread through London society. The Duke of Strathaven had been effusive in his appreciation and thankfulness for Robert's actions and Robert had reveled in it, finding that his newfound status within the *ton* was something to be enjoyed. He had assumed that it would continue into this Season and had told himself that, once he was at a ball or soiree with the ladies of the *ton*, his exaltation would continue. "The Duke and Duchess were, of course, very grateful," he finished, as Lord Burnley nodded slowly, although there was no exclamation of surprise on his lips nor a gasp of astonishment. "The gentlemen of London are likely a little envious of me, of course, but that is to be expected."

Much to his astonishment, Lord Burnley broke out into laughter at this statement, his eyes crinkling and his hand lifting his still-full glass towards Robert.

"Indeed, I am certain they are," he replied, his words filled with a sarcasm that could not be missed. "Good evening, Lord Crampton. I shall go now and tell the other gentlemen here in White's precisely who you are and what you have done. No doubt they shall come to speak to you at once, given your great and esteemed situation."

Robert set his jaw, his eyes a little narrowed as he watched Lord Burnley step away, all too aware of the man's cynicism. *It does not matter,* he told himself, firmly. *Lord Burnley, too, will be a little jealous of your success, and your standing in the* ton. *What else should you expect other than sarcasm and rebuttal?*

Rising to his feet, Robert set his shoulders and, with his head held high, made his way from White's, trying to ignore the niggle of doubt that entered his mind. Tomorrow, he told himself, he would find things much more improved. He would go to whatever occasion he wished and would find himself, of course, just as he had been last Season – practically revered by all those around him.

He could hardly wait.

CHECK out the rest of the story in the Kindle store. More Than a Companion

JOIN MY MAILING LIST

Sign up for my newsletter to stay up to date on new releases, contests, giveaways, freebies, and deals!

Free book with signup!

Facebook Giveaways! Books and Amazon gift cards! Join me on Facebook: https://www.facebook.com/rosepearsonauthor

Website: www.RosePearsonAuthor.com

Follow me on Goodreads: Author Page

You can also follow me on Bookbub! Click on the picture below – see the Follow button?

214 | JOIN MY MAILING LIST

Printed in Dunstable, United Kingdom